Devour

A SAPPHIC MONSTER ROMANCE

DAE STORM

Acknowledgements

To my little group of local writer friends, you know who you are, thank you for putting up with me and my late night shenanigans.

To M, my darling, for always telling me you're proud of me even on the days I've only written one word!

I'd like to thank the "Monster Manor" Discord server specifically and all of the wonderful friends I've made there for supporting me and cheering me on the entire time I worked on this book. It truly means so much to me to have such a friendly and frankly, feral, group of people to share my work and time with.

Contents

To all the exhausted queers and allies who wish they could run away into the arms of a 8ft tall monster with a forked tongue and never have to work or pay rent again.
This is for you.

Authors Note - CWs

Devour is a monster romance with many *explicit dark and seductive themes* but it does *not* contain noncon. That said, as with the very idea of monster/prey, the potential dubious nature of the relationship is up for debate. Below is a list of possible content warnings some may want to read. If you feel there any missing that should be there please do not hesitate to contact me. A list of *kinks* can be found on my website. (https://d-author.link/)

If you are not interested in content warnings or do not want certain acts spoiled, please continue on without reading them.

- kidnapping (temporary) (on page)

- unwanted restraint (temporary) (on page)

- death of parent (previous) (mentioned)

- anxiety/fear (on page)

- chronic pain (mentioned) (on page)

- cheating (not main couple) (mentioned)

- death (minor characters) (mentioned)

- graphic death (minor character) (on page)

- explicit sexual content (on page)

- graphic violence (minor characters) (on page)

- blood drinking (on page)

- torture by side character (moderate) (on page)

- lasting effects of torture (mentioned) (on page)

- forced feeding for nutrition (once) (on page)

- abuse by parent (mentioned)

- accidental neglect of pet (mentioned) (on page)

- arachnid (spider) side character (on page)

- war (mentioned)

- dementia (mentioned)

- hunting humans (mentioned) (on page)

- physically eating humans (mentioned)

- emotion and soul eating (on page)

1

THE CHASE, THE GRAB, AND THE LACK OF EXPLANATION

Renee

Who was I to think I could ever have a birthday that didn't end in a fucking headache for me?

Three years ago, on my birthday, my drunk cousin had fallen right into my special ordered birthday cake. Two years ago, the restaurant had written the reservation wrong; and one year ago my father announced his engagement to a twenty-year-old model only a few years after my mother's passing.

This year? Well, this year topped them all.

Anger heated my body as I stomped through the pouring rain that rolled down my bare shoulders and soaked my hair. Between that and the tears in my eyes, I could hardly see, but I didn't care. I'd make it home one way or another.

In the dark of the night, with my pantyhose clad feet slapping through puddle after puddle, I felt no fear.

"Asshole," I growled through clenched teeth. My heels dangled haphazardly from my fingers as I tramped carelessly. It didn't matter that the hem of my strapless dress was completely soiled or that there was definitely a pebble caught under my foot.

As I reached the corner of the street, I took a fleeting glance behind me. I barely saw the neon sign above the door of the club.

If I never saw that damn sign again, I'd be happy.

"Motherfucker," I hissed. My tongue darted along the rest of the crimson color on my plump lips. With hunched shoulders, I continued walking.

"Who breaks up with someone on their birthday?"

My empty hand balled into a fist. "Screw Uber. I don't need anyone. Not Kevin and not Casey. Bitch." I snarled. Kevin didn't even have the decency to say *'it's not you, it's me'*. No, it was all me.

Too needy. Clingy. Stubborn. Opinionated.

Crazy.

I ground my teeth. I hated that word, but if it wasn't for the bouncer in the club, I would've shown him crazy. Lucky for him, he'd just have to pick his shit up off the sidewalk after I was done with it.

I knew not putting him on the lease was a good idea.

I swallowed hard and stopped near the bus stop, but I didn't duck into the small shelter with a bench. I just stood there. There wasn't a soul around me and I was glad. I didn't need anyone asking me what was wrong as mascara dripped down my face and my curly hair drooped tangled around my head.

My throat was tight as I thought about Kevin. I wanted to tell myself I didn't care about him, but that wasn't true.

"Four fucking years," I spoke into the rain. "Four years I gave that dick." My jaw felt as though it might shatter. The ache in my chest was so bad I wished I could rip my heart out just like he did. Most of all, I wanted to scream.

I had shared myself with him. Showed him parts of me no one

else knew, and he'd told me they were the reason he didn't want to be with me. That fucking hurt. Most of all, seeing him look at my best friend the way he used to look at me... As though she was different, that she wouldn't be *'too much'* for him.

I'd been too much and yet not enough my entire life. Too sassy, too promiscuous, too queer, but not queer *enough*. Never enough, always too much.

I looked down and saw that my hands were shaking and I had an iron grip on my heels. My stomach was so tight. The heat that radiated my emotion caused the icy rain to steam from my skin.

Standing in the middle of the sidewalk, I lost it.

A strained closed mouth scream blared from my throat and forced my mouth open. The sound echoed around me in the downpour. I threw myself toward the bricked wall of a nearby building and hurled my heels against it.

"Fuck!" I yelled, "fucking, motherfucker fuck!" I slammed my heels and free fist against the wall against and again. The course brick scraping and nicking my skin. "I'm crazy?!" I hissed.

Tears leaked from my eyes, but I couldn't tell where they started and the rain ended. My face was so hot that it hurt and my head pounded, blood rushing to my ringing ears.

I felt like I was on fire and the need to release the burning inside me was so intense that I was dizzy. I tilted my head backward and screamed. My knees shivered underneath me.

"Shit." I panted. I let go of the battered heels and let my nails scrape against the brick.

I swallowed the lump in my throat as I turned around, and I saw several lights flip on in the apartments across the street. Oh well.

The rain had let up. I looked at my hands. Every couple of seconds, the rain would wash away the blood that oozed out of my scratched and speckled hands..

My throat was sore, but my chest and shoulders were lighter. I felt less tense despite the tears that were still flowing. Several lights flicked off as I walked again. The last thing I needed was someone asking me if I was okay. I didn't have it in me to lie.

However, as I walked along in the drizzling weather, I felt a presence. A nervous bubble flipped around in my stomach. The kind that I always got when I felt like I was being followed. The air rather suddenly heated around me and became overwhelmingly heavy.

"What?" I mumbled. I felt the urge to look over my shoulder, but I resisted. Said shoulders pulled up to my ears again and my bare feet slapped against the pavement quicker. I'd left my heels behind entirely.

I whirled toward an alley that I knew was open-ended and something caught my vision. Someone caught my vision. At first, I wasn't sure what I was seeing. It happened in an instant. The creature was tall and loomed in the alleyway's darkness, the streetlights on the other side just barely illuminated them. I blinked, but when my eyes focused again, they were gone.

"That...didn't happen." I had to have been seeing things. But a vision of glowing red eyes pouring into mine from the darkness flooded my thoughts.

When I turned back around after deciding I didn't want to go that way after all, my thought of seeing things was completely overturned.

A creature towered over me, as dark as coal, and red eyes glaring at me from above.

"Run," they growled.

They didn't have to tell me twice. I took no second glances as I turned again and headed down the long alleyway. Hard pebbles and cracks in the pavement nicked the soles of my feet, but I ran faster. My purse swung and wobbled along my shoulder and I caught the strap in my hand as it slid off. I held it in my hand tightly. I could use it as a weapon if needed. But what good would it do against something so...massive?

My heart was racing. Everything seemed like a blur around me, the only thing I could focus on was the streetlight on the other side. I couldn't scream. Nothing would come out of my mouth but air. If I wanted to run, I needed to keep my breath as steady as possible. I'd never run so fast in my life.

I felt them behind me. Hot. It was like heat radiated in waves from them. Every so often, it would switch to the left, to the right.

Some part of me was positive if I could just make it a little longer, everything would be okay. Stopping was not an option.

A growl sounded behind me and elicited something unexpected within me. Pure excitement. I had never felt so alive in that moment. As the heat from this monster's body heated my own, and their claws scraped against the ground, every part of my body was alive and on fire.

Invigorated, I made a left turn down the street without stopping or looking to see what was really ahead of me.

Suddenly, the creature was in front of me. My heels scraped on the sidewalk, aching and bleeding. They growled down at me, their eyes glowing brighter than even before. So close, I could smell them. Musky and woodsy.

Every nerve in my body lit up like a live wire. It was clear that I had not truly been out running them. They had been letting me.

"Delicious." The word rumbled out from them in the surrounding dimness.

My knees locked up underneath me, and I could not run.

Their large, dark clawed hands reached out and gripped me.

Then everything went dark.

When the blackness turned to consciousness, the first thing I noticed was the ache in my arms. My fuzzy mind struggled to process where I was, even as my senses took in everything bit by bit. It was so dark that the only way I could tell my eyes were open was the feeling of my false lashes against the very tops of my cheeks when I blinked. I grunted as I shifted my body. My arms were stuck above my head, wrists held together by something thick and rough textured. I suspected a rope.

Despite the dimness of the room, it wasn't cold or cool at all. Sweat slowly dripped down from my hairline and between my breasts. I was sure I was still wearing my dress, but I couldn't see a single thing when I tilted my head down.

I groaned at the uncomfortable stretch of my neck and shoulders. "What the fuck?" I huffed.

It had to be a dream. All of it. That was the only thing that made sense.

I squeezed my eyes closed, desperately trying to wake myself up. But the straining of my muscles and pounding of my heart in my rib cage continued. There was no waking up.

As I squirmed, my eyes burned. Was I going to be left here in the darkness to starve and dehydrate? Panic rose from my lungs and I found myself calling out into the dark. "Help!"

"Hello!?" I yelled. "Anyone, please!"

No answer. I hung there, tip toes on the ground, for what felt like forever as the frustration built up inside me.

"If you're going to leave me here to die, at least show your fucking face!" I hissed out. Tears dripped from my eyes and rolled down my hot face.

My head felt so dizzy I could barely stand it. Sweat drip, drip, dripped down every inch of me. Soaking into my hair and the fabric that clung tightly to my body. My stomach heaved as I only seemed to get hotter with the rising anxiety. I fought against my bindings.

"Let me out!" I yelled. "Can't...breathe." I sucked in a breath despite my words. The air was so thick that it seemed I'd need to take twenty breaths to get the effects of one.

Light flooded the room as the door creaked open. I squinted as my eyes adjusted to the light, and my pulse raced faster as the towering figure who had chased me came into view. Glowing red eyes poured into mine, piercing and bringing goosebumps to life on my skin.

"What do you w-want?!" I asked, shifting my body as far back as I could, my toes struggled to touch the floor.

The monster got closer, claws reaching out for me, and I screamed as they ripped at my clothing. Tearing at the fabric with sharp nails in haphazard motions that somehow didn't cut my skin. Their large hands gripped at me so tightly that I could feel the heat, even hotter than the room, that emanated from them.

"Stop moving," they growled.

My body responded in a way I didn't expect with a hard shiver at the sound of their guttural voice. Still, I squirmed in an attempt to get out of their grasp.

"I'm trying to help!" Their voice grew louder.

As the last scraps of my clothing fell to the floor, I hung there naked and bare for the creature before me to see. Every inch of me was coated in a sheen of sweat.

I quickly realized that I wasn't as swelteringly hot anymore. Every now and again, a slight breeze hit my skin and cooled the moisture that clung to it.

"Don't touch me," I mumbled weakly. My limbs felt heavy along with their ache, and my head tired.

"Quiet," they replied.

I looked up and realized just how far they towered above me. They were so close that I could smell them. A musky scent that filled my senses, and something else that I couldn't quite grasp.

My eyes adjusted to the dim light further, and their red eyes seemed to illuminate more of their features.

My pulse quickened as I took their face in. Their skin was an unnatural red, that was lined by patches of pitch black fur. Their nose distinctly feline, as well as their eyes, and their mouth with thin black lips held a stark line of sharp teeth.

"W-What are you?" I choked out.

The monster before me rumbled out a response that I was certain portrayed annoyance.

They started to turn around, but I spat out another response.

"You have me tied up here. You could at least tell me who the fuck you are!" I thrashed with all the strength I could muster up, feeling the rope pull and burn at my wrists and hands.

They lunge forward at me and my entire body went rigid, my knees bumping each other. I squeezed my eyes shut.

"You're lucky I haven't swallowed you whole yet." They were much closer to my face than before. I could feel their breath on the side of my neck and face, it was warm against my fluttering pulse.

My hips twitched forward slightly, and I groaned.

"Just get it over with." I swallowed my fear. "You could at least give me your name before I die."

I opened my eyes and looked directly into the face of my captor with no hesitation. I was too tired to be scared, any more screaming or flailing, and I was sure to pass out from exhaustion.

"You're not going to beg for your life?" they asked, looking at me so intently that it made me even hotter than I already was.

I licked my dry lips.

"Who are you?" I asked again.

The monster groaned an indistinct sound and suddenly their face was against my head, inhaling, and moving farther down.

"You smell so...succulent," they hummed, no, purred.

As they sunk lower, I felt the vibration against my stomach, so close to my naked groin, and I squeezed my thighs together. I should be afraid, and my heart was still beating hard in my chest, but I felt something else at the closeness of this creature of nightmares.

As my eyes focused on them more intently, I could see strips of dark fabric, leather perhaps, banded around the monster's chest, that I now realized was more akin to human than feline in its round bust.

Was the monster a woman?

Before I could think for more than a second or two, something hot and soft pushed against my thighs and I looked down to see the monster's nose. They pressed it just above my pussy, before moving down along the apex and curve of my thigh and hip.

My breath caught as she purred against my flesh.

I wiggled against her, denying myself the arousal that was crawling up my spine.

"Get away!" I insisted, pushing my toes against the hard floor to move myself back.

She rose to her feet, towering above me once more. Her movements were so quick that I flinched.

"You can't smell me if I don't know your name!" I panted. Not realizing how breathless I was until that moment.

"Why does it matter, human?" She asked, irritation lacing her rumbly voice.

I squeezed my bound hands into fists and my brows knit together. "Ex-fucking-cuse me if I'd like to know the name of the monster who chased me down, kidnapped me, and has me hanging from the fucking ceiling! I'm so sorry that I don't want you smelling my cunt when I don't even know why I'm here, who you are! I should just hang here limp and let you do whatever you want!" I snarled out in a string of huffs and squirmed my body hard with each word, frustration exploding out of me.

I wasn't afraid anymore, but I sure as hell wasn't going to go out without a fight.

The monster's eyes only glowed brighter at my words, and she moved close once again. I jerked away from her as much as I could. She reached out and her claws pressed into the bare flesh of my hips.

As she leaned in to my ear, my head went dizzy.

"You smell even better when you're so angry, Little One," she growled, "fuck it's so hard not to devour you."

I opened my mouth to swear at her, but what came out instead surprised me.

"Then do it." My voice was almost a whine.

Her claws pressed into me harder, stinging at the very edges of pain, and I shivered.

"If you want to kill me, devour me, why don't you just do it?" I asked.

I watched as her pink tongue, long and forked at the end, eased out and licked at her sharp teeth. Mesmerized, I watched it for a brief second, wondering just how sharp her teeth were. If they would cut me with just a simple touch, or how much pressure would need to be applied?

"You'd be gone if I took all of you," she growled, "then I'd never get to smell you or taste you again." She moved back and away from me.

I found myself aching in her absence, and couldn't help but wonder...

How fucked up am I?

I tilted my head down and closed my eyes. All the energy that I had was gone for the moment. I was hanging there, hot, wet, and utterly confused by the situation and my reaction to it.

Just as I was preparing myself to be left where I was, with no answers, the monster spoke up in a quieter tone.

"Hale, that is who I am."

2

THE HORNY DILEMMA

Renee

"Your name is Hale?" I asked. I tilted my head back, and I fixed my eyes up, looking into her inhuman face. Hale responded with a grunt, which I interpreted as a 'yes'.

I swallowed hard as my gaze landed once again on her body that was a combination of blood red skin, night black fur, and feminine curves that mimicked my own. The bands of leather hid only her breasts and groin, like a medieval bikini. I found myself uncertain of my assumption of gender, after all, Hale was a monster whose existence I didn't understand.

Before I spoke, I took a deep breath, trying to calm my racing heart. I felt a strange sense of intrigue along with my anxiety when I looked at Hale.

"Are you..." I searched for the right word, "a woman?" I asked. Even I wasn't so sure that the term was correct. I knew nothing about Hale, making a guess based on my society's construct of gender. One that I was already certain couldn't possibly encompass the creature before me.

"I'm *mardan*," Hale replied, "the closest to you would be female. Woman..." She tilted her head to the side. "Yes, but not quite. Human labels have much more personal meaning."

I furrowed my brow, processing Hale's words. "So you're closest to a female human, but don't care what you're called?" I asked, clarifying.

Hale growled quietly and moved closer. I noticed the way she seemed to twitch each time she inhaled. Her eyes grew darker.

"You are a woman?" Hale asked.

I found I hesitated for a moment. "Yes," I replied.

"Then you may call me the same," she said.

I exhaled slowly. "Why haven't you killed me?" I asked, "why are we talking about this?" I was strung up from the ceiling, naked, covered in sweat and waiting for the shoe to drop.

Hale groaned and raked her claws through the fur at the sides of her face.

"Trust me, I want to," she huffed at me. "I have to." Her wide shoulders rolled back, and she moved even closer to me. I could feel her warm breath against the side of my face. I shivered and closed my eyes, preparing for the worst.

"Why?" I asked. "If I'm going to die, at least tell me why you did this?"

"You saw me," Hale told me, voice rough and low, "you had to be captured."

I squeezed my eyes shut tighter as I felt her presence grow closer, her claws press into the sides of my thighs.

"You are a danger to me, to others."

My eyes shot open at those words. "What?" I blurted out, a bubble of laughter stuck in my stomach, "danger, to you!?"

My eyes burned. "I barely saw you," I insisted, "and it's fucking hilarious that you think I could be a danger to you!" I squirmed, feeling the frustration building up inside me once again. "You seriously captured me for this?"

I panted for air as I struggled. The more I worked myself up, the hotter Hale's eyes burned into me. Her shoulders labored and her height seemed even more menacing than before.

"That can't be it." I wrinkled my reddened face. "You want something else," I insisted.

I remembered how she'd told me I was delicious, smelled delicious. The way she seemed to get more agitated the closer she was to me.

"What aren't you telling me?" I asked louder, putting as much energy as I could into it. I was so hungry, thirsty. I didn't know how long I'd been there. But I knew Hale wasn't telling me everything, and I'd be damned if I died for a split second glance in the dark of the night.

"Fuck," Hale growled, leaning down farther, until her face was so close to mine that just a slight move caused my cheeks to brush against the tips of her fur. "The more worked up you get, the more I feel you," she told me. "The more I want you."

I felt the pointed tips of her claws press into me harder and my thighs squeezed together in response. All I could manage was the low hum of a word. "What?"

She turned her head and pressed her face into the crook of my neck. "I heard your scream," she told me. "I felt your passion, and anger, sadness. I felt your emotion so strong. So...decadent." The pointed tips of her tongue glided along my neck for just a split second. Wet and slightly rough.

My entire body trembled.

"What do you want with me?" I asked.

I felt her inhale and exhale against my skin. "So much," she whispered.

Her claws stung at my thighs, but it only sent my head reeling. I found myself more aroused than I had been in years. As her sharp teeth grazed my bare shoulder, I was more roused than I had been with anyone, even Kevin. Who only hours or perhaps the day before, I had thought I wanted to marry.

I whimpered, a sound that I had never made before in my life.

Suddenly, Hale moved away from me and I heard a ripping above my head before I fell to the hard floor. The rope that had once been secured around my wrists was left dangling above. I lowered myself more against the floor, that was cooler than the air around me.

Letting it soothe the heat within me.

"Get it over with," I mumbled. Waning back and forth between fighting for my life and just lying on the floor. My energy seemed to come in bursts, and at that moment, I was just tired. My muscles relaxed now that I wasn't hanging from the ceiling, trying to keep myself steady with the tips of my toes.

I cracked open my eyes to see Hale standing several feet from me. She was even more daunting from this angle, like a skyscraper. She seemed to be debating, or hesitant.

Suddenly she disappeared from my view, from the room entirely. The door shut, and it was pitch black again. How long was she going to leave me here this time?

My breath grew shallow as I laid on the floor with my eyes fixed on where I knew the door was. I fought the urge to fall asleep, feeling a desire to keep myself awake in the face of the situation I was in.

Just when I thought Hale wasn't going to return soon, the door creaked open. I squinted into the light that washed over the room. My eyes slid up Hales clawed feet to her glowing eyes that burned so hot it made my entire body tense.

"Get up," Hale told me.

I struggled at first to push up from the floor. I panted as I stood up, keeping my eyes on her. I noticed that there was something bundled up in her hands.

"You wear this." Hale tossed the bundle of fabric at me. A soft cream-colored fabric, thin but heavier than expected.

"It will keep you cooler," she said.

I felt her eyes on me. It was both exciting and anxiety inducing at the same tie. I faltered anxiously on my feet.

"Staying for the show?" I asked sarcastically. Asked the literal monster before me.

Hale grunted softly and looked at me even more heatedly, but then turned and left the room. There was a scratching on the floor as she placed something down to hold the massive door open just a few inches.

I swallowed hard as I stared at the small opening in the door, then looked down at the fabric in my arms. As I unfurled it, I realized it was a dress, but it wasn't exactly sewn together. The fabric, soft and thin, was pulled and knotted together at the sides with a long skirt with slits on either side. The top was loose bands of fabric that I had to place over my chest and shoulders, then fasten behind my neck. The remaining fabric draped behind me. It seemed to soak in my sweat and cool me off better than my dress had. As I looked at the dress in the beam of light from the door, the color seemed to shift slightly with my movements. The cream color swirling with various shades of white in no discernible pattern or way that made sense.

My brows furrowed, and I looked up at the door again. I hesitantly stepped closer and realized just how huge the door was. What I had thought was a couple inches of space open to let light in was closer to a foot of space. My breath caught in my throat, and I was no longer curious about the dress.

I stretched my body as far as I could without touching the door and turned my head. I expected to see Hale outside the door, but all I could see was the gray stone hallway. My pulse quickened as I realized I was alone.

I had no idea where I was. I could be one thousand miles from home, or ten miles. What if it was my only chance? Was I seriously debating if I should try to get away?

What was wrong with me...Of course I needed to get out. Who would feed my cat, Fern, if I wasn't there?

I held my breath as I made my decision and squeezed through the opening of the door. I held myself steady against the heavy door, feeling the weight of it against my palms but not pushing it any further for fear that it would make noise.

Surely Hale could hear me anyhow? I brushed the thought away, focusing only on getting out of the room. I ignored the ache in my stomach and limbs.

My heart was so loud in my ears that it caused me to be paranoid that Hale could hear it, too. Still, when she didn't come barreling down the hallway, the second my bare feet touched down, I felt a slight relief. And oddly enough, disappointment.

After hesitating for just that moment, I urged my legs forward and moved left down the hallway. I had no idea where I was going, but there had to be some way out. As I grew more eager to escape the prison I was in, my movements grew more erratic and less cautious. Louder. Drawing even more possible attention to me.

I made it around another corner, thinking I was perhaps making my way to an exit, but it seemed to go on forever.

Suddenly I felt an oh so familiar heat behind me. I urged myself to run faster, despite knowing it was fruitless. My hands grasped at the makeshift dress around me, holding it up higher to avoid tripping over it, but the fabric kept slipping out of my hands. I narrowly avoided slipping as I rounded another corner.

"Run, Little One!" Hale growled behind me. The sound rounding back into a guttural laugh that sent chills up every inch of my body. Exhilarated, I pushed myself forward faster, and panted painfully for each breath.

I knew she was after me, that she would catch me, there was no out running a monster, and yet I kept going. I slammed into the corner of a wall as I tried to turn yet again, and groaned in pain as I was momentarily stopped.

"I'll always catch you," she breathed against the back of my neck. So close to me. Still, I tossed my body forward, overwhelmed by the blood pumping faster through my veins. Every part of my body was tingling, and I felt as though I was a wick lit by a match.

As I struggled for air the longer I went, a strained, breathless laugh escaped my chest. Surprising me as I came to what I was certain was another endlessly long hallway.

"Do you like this?" Hale huffed. My feet slapped against the floor, but hers were eerily silent.

Did I?

It didn't matter. I came stumbling to a stop as I looked ahead and realized the hallway was a dead end. Two doors. One on the left, one on the right, but nothing ahead of me.

My vision was going blurry, and my lungs were burning. My legs two wobbling noodles of exhaustion.

Hale gripped me from behind and her claws against my stomach. The heat of her body pressed against me through the thin fabric that clung to my damp skin.

"I can hear you, always," she rumbled into my ear, "...smell you. Feel every move you make. Your running tortures me, Little One. Delightfully."

As her voice grew lower and her touch firmer, I knew without a doubt this turned me on. How or why didn't matter right then.

Her touch moved lower, resting against my pubis, the pads of her clawed hands resting ever so slightly above my wet pussy.

A whine bubbled up and out of my mouth. My head was so dizzy.

Hale tsked at me. "You're only making it harder for me..." Her free hand moved my hair away from my shoulder and neck.

I felt her forked tongue drag along the back of my neck, and I shivered hard.

My body jostled as my knees gave out underneath me, and her hold tightened.

"Perhaps I should feed you."

That was the last thing I heard before everything faded into a low hum of energy.

3

THE ONE WITH DESSERT

Hale

The sight before me made my mouth water. I'd tied the small human to a chair, and the ropes pressed deliciously against her soft, curvy body. My ears perked as I watched her begin to rouse. Her breath caught and her pulse quickened.

Renee squirmed as she came too, and my hunger grew with each second that passed. I crouched in front of her with my head tilted down and scanned her crinkling face with my eyes.

"Mm." She made a sound as her tired eyes fluttered open.

A rumbling vibrated along my sternum and throat as I watched her and waited.

I was still reeling from the chase. Every part of this human seemed to call to me, and the darkness begged me to swallow her soul whole. She had been trying to escape, despite knowing she could not outrun me. I had felt her emotions charged in the air all around us.

Fear, excitement...lust.

"Little one," I purred to her to wake her further.

I could not resist reaching a claw out and tilting her sagging head up to look into my face. Her breath washed out against my skin and fur. Her scent was utterly intoxicating. The fire within burned hotter.

"Oh, hell…" Renee muttered, her voice raspier than before. My eyes flitted to her mouth, watching her light pink tongue dart along her dry lips, and I noticed for the first time the lack of moisture in her mouth.

"Thirsty?" I asked her, curious.

I had only ever watched humans from afar and taken them for only as long as it took to end them. Never had I been so close to a living one for this long.

"I thought it was a dream," she replied. Her eyes were open full now, looking at me with uncertainty. I felt the warmth of her emotions flooding the room. Even now, she was hot with desire. Though our hungers surely were different.

"Not a nightmare?" I moved my face closer, tilting my head to the side. Desperate to be closer to her. Her energy pulled me in, so much stronger than any other.

My eyes moved quickly down her body as her stomach growled loudly.

"That chase worked you up," I commented. I watched her face grow darker with blush at the double meaning of my words.

"I wouldn't be hungry…if you hadn't kidnapped me," she huffed out.

It seemed the rest she'd gotten, however short, had reignited her strength to fight against any desire she was feeling.

I couldn't help but grin at her, my mouth pulled up wide at the corners and bearing my sharp teeth. My teeth glinted in the reflection of her eyes, and her body went stiff.

"Let me feed you," I said. It was not a suggestion.

"Why? So you can fatten me up to eat me?" she asked.

I growled low as I stood up fully. "I could end you now if I wished," I reminded her.

Renee's brow furrowed tighter, and she squirmed against her bindings.

"Then just get it over with," she hissed at me. "You want me...then take me."

I shivered and resisted the urge to do just that.

"You perplex me, Little One," I purred at her, leaning back down to place my face beside hers. I nuzzle my nose against her cheek and inhale.

"Your scent drives me wild, I want to devour you each time your heart beats," I told her as my sound vibrated against her skin. "...but something is different with you."

I pulled back and saw her staring at me. "What do you mean?"

I licked my teeth. "Your energy calls to me. It's so strong. You burn so hot."

The confusion did not leave her face, but her legs and thighs squeezed together.

I could smell her arousal, wet and warm. My cunt throbbed between my legs and I forced myself to turn around to the table several feet away.

On the table was a plate I had secured with a dark red dripping dessert. It was sickeningly sweet and bitter all in the same, and most humans did not enjoy the taste, but it would fill Renee and give her strength. I grabbed some with one of my claws, tucked in the crooked of my finger, and turned back around to her. The dessert dripped slowly to the floor.

"Eat, Little One," I insisted and held it out to her.

Renee eyed my hand and the food within. "What is that?" she asked, sniffing and her nose scrunched slightly. "C-Cake?"

"Eat it, it will fuel you."

She struggled against her bindings as she attempted to lean closer. "I can't get silverware?" She muttered.

I growled as I lost patience and grabbed her chin with my other hand, forcing my clawed finger into her mouth with just enough pressure not to hurt her; but I saw the sudden fear in her eyes right before I did it.

I pulled my claw out of her mouth; it glistened with her saliva and remnants of the sticky sweet substance. Renee's face scrunched up and she spit the food out at me with no hesitation.

My thick blood boiled as I looked at her. Her chin and lips were sticky. A growl rumbled low in my chest and I glared back at her.

"For a girl who doesn't want to die, you're making it hard not to end you," I told her.

Renee squirmed against her bindings again and wiggled the chair. "I can feed myself," she insisted, "...you'll just hurt me."

I barked out a laugh, turned around and grabbed another finger full of food before turning back to her.

"Eat," I outstretched my arm.

She clamped her mouth shut in a line that was slightly down turned. Her brows knit, and her body was stiff in defiance.

Oh, the fire that she lit within me was scorching and I could hardly bear it.

"Fine." I crouched down to be face to face with her, and licked the food from my claw, but did not chew nor swallow. Its taste was a faded bitter sweet to me. Spongy and sticky. But it was not what I craved, nor what I needed.

Renee's eyes were on my maw and she was salivating, I could see it build up as her tongue crossed her plump bottom lip.

With only the barest hesitation, I leaned in until our mouths were connected, hers much smaller than my own. My teeth nipped at her flesh, but I only stayed long enough to sway the food from my mouth into hers with my long tongue. Her breath became a trapped moan of a sound in her throat.

I pulled back and forced her jaw closed with my hand.

Her eyes were wide and her hands fists, but the scent of her arousal was more potent than before.

"Swallow," I demanded.

She stared at me and did as I asked. I watched her throat move, and my gaze shifted to her pulse. Quick, but not as strong as it could be.

I looked her in the eyes. "When I want to hurt you, I will," I said, "...do not pretend it does not make you wet."

Her face, so round and soft, flushed dark, and she gawked at me. "W-What?" she asked.

I licked at my lips and tasted her there. The taste of her mouth was so unique to her, unlike any other creature I had kissed or feasted upon. To describe was beyond my senses, and all I knew was that I wanted more.

"I smell your desire," I told her and leaned my head down farther, lowering my shoulders. "I feel your want."

I rubbed my face along her thigh and drew a line inward to her abdomen, just above her hot, pulsing pussy. I had never tasted a human's, but knew that they were not so different from my own.

Renee whimpered, and her thighs clenched.

"H-How?" she asked, her voice quiet and breathless.

Despite how strong her desire was, I sensed she was attempting to change the subject, to ignore it.

My desire to devour her in more ways than I could count was overwhelming. How I had not ended her life already had been a mystery to me, but I was seeing it now.

"How what?" I ask her, though I know. "How are you alive?" I couldn't help but smirk into the fabric at her thighs.

It took all of my strength to pull myself up and away from her lap, looking into her face once more.

She swallowed hard. "Yes, but..." she looked away from my gaze, "...how do you smell me?" She shook her head, confusion and curiosity mixed in her eyes.

I tilted my head to the side and breathed in deeply. Her smell invaded my senses, and I purred quietly. Unable to stop myself.

"First. My hunger for your life isn't as strong as my hunger for your body, it seems." I bare my teeth. "Second. It is my nature. How do you smell flowers?"

Renee squeezed her eyes shut. "If you're going to keep me here, I deserve to know more."

I stood up fully and grabbed more of the food, and held it out to her. "You eat, I tell."

She looked at my hand and pursed her lips. "What is it? It tastes...like chocolate, almost."

"Eat." I did not answer her question.

Renee sighed, but her tongue reached out and she took a bite of the food in my palm. She chewed and looked up at me expectantly, her head tilted back.

"I told you, I smell and sense your fear. Your excitement, sadness, desire," I explained, "...but what you feel is so much stronger than any other human I have hunted."

She swallowed. "You hunt humans?"

I motioned for her to continue eating, and she did so hesitantly. Each chew came with a slight look of distaste, but she ate.

"I must eat too." I looked away from her. The sight of her tongue darting out to catch crumbs was distracting me.

"You...eat us?" she continued.

"Your emotions, and your life. Your soul."

4

BONDING

Renee

The sickly sweet substance in my mouth was growing on me. It filled my empty stomach, and I felt less dizzy with each bite from Hale's hand. Though as Hale spoke of what her own meals were, she was salivating.

I shivered, and I wasn't sure if it was fear or interest. Knowing she could smell how aroused I was strange. I didn't want to admit it. Could I really be so turned on by this creature? Monster?

The chase, the hunt, it was the most exhilarating thing I had ever felt; but was dying worth it?

"...and you want to eat my soul?" I asked, stupidly. Of course she did. She was just buttering me up so that I'd be even more tasty for her dinner of Horny Twenty Something Life Force.

I squirmed against the ropes tying me to the massive chair. My feet were nowhere near touching the floor. I stopped, however, as Hale stared off beside my head for a long moment.

"I don't know," she replied.

I blinked. "You don't know?" I tilted my head back as far as possible just to look up at her.

She motioned for me to continue eating, and I did so. Not minding it as much. Though, I still wondered what the hell it was.

"Your emotions are so much stronger. I want to taste them, taste you. It could feed me deeply," she husked out.

My thighs squeezed together even harder, and I struggled to breathe. "Why don't you?"

What the fuck was I doing? Asking? Wanting?

Hale groaned and slammed her now empty but sticky hand on the table behind her.

"I don't know that I could control myself."

I watched her back and shoulders move up and down with her heavy breaths as she faced away from me. She was more than just big and tall. She was strong. Even in the areas that were covered in pitch black fur, I could see the outlines of her muscles. My gaze traveled down to her rear, where a long pointed feline tail flowed out from a hole in the back of her leather garment. I found myself curious about it, and about the parts of her I could not see.

She had told me that was aroused by me, that she wanted me. Not quite in those words, but I understood what she had said. Her desire to fuck me was stronger than her desire to kill me, but she was resisting both, it seemed.

My face and body flushed hotter, and I looked away from her.

What was I thinking?

She was a monster who had kidnapped me and was holding me captive. The only thing I should've been thinking about was how to get away, or perhaps question my beliefs in religion and ask to be saved before it would be too late.

I swallowed thickly. Still tasting the strange, potential dessert in my mouth.

It was true; she was a monster, but she had just been feeding me from her hand. Her clawed and dangerous hand.

My hips twitched, and I looked down at them incredulously before looking back up at Hale. Up and up.

She still hadn't turned around.

"Tell me...more about you. About where I am," I insisted, "am I in another country?"

My question elicited a low laugh of a sound from Hale and she finally turned around. "More like another world, Little One."

That nickname...it made my core ache in ways I didn't know were possible; but my head quickly caught up with what she had just said.

"What?" I asked, staring.

"You are in the Midaworld," she told me as she stepped closer.

I shook my head. "...I'm on another planet?"

"No, not exactly a different planet," Hale said.

My face contorts, eyebrows as knit as my stomach suddenly was. "I'm in another world, but not another planet?" I pursed my lips. "Like, the underworld, or hell? Or heaven?" I chewed on my bottom lip as I tried to mull through this. Until then I hadn't believed in any of those, but if this place existed, those could too. Right?

"Something like those," Hale replied.

My heart jumped up into my throat. How long had I been there? Oh, poor Fern...

I squirmed in my seat; the ropes rubbing uncomfortably against me, but the pressure having a calming effect. "I can't be here," I said, "in this...what did you call it?"

"Midaworld," she repeated.

"Tell me about it. About you. Are there more like you?" I asked. I needed to know more. My head was spinning with the possibilities. What else existed that I didn't know about? Who was going to take care of Fern? How long had I been there? How many messages and calls had I missed and was anyone looking for me?

I couldn't get those questions out of my mouth, it was all too much. It was easier to focus on getting more information about Hale and this other world I was in.

But Hale just looked at me, not answering me.

"You've already said I have to die because I saw you," I reminded her, "what's the harm in explaining this shit to me?"

I narrowed my eyes, trying to decide if I even believed that she would kill me. Not that I didn't believe she couldn't, but... she didn't want to. Not as much as she wanted to keep me alive. As much as she wanted to fuck me.

I quivered again at the thought. What would that even be like? I forced myself away from those thoughts as she spoke.

"Midaworld is full of demons that cannot walk freely in your world," she told me. "Others like my kind, yes, we feed on emotions and souls. Others feed on blood and flesh, bone."

I recoiled slightly as she bared her teeth, but could not look away from the sharp glistening points. She certainly looked as though she should feed on blood and bone.

"But you don't eat flesh?" I asked.

Hale's forked tongue peaked out for a split second. "I can. It does not fill me the same. Full but empty. Blood...I crave it occasionally."

Goosebumps covered my body. I licked my own lips to wet them, my mouth suddenly dry.

"Killing me for seeing you," I started, "it's a rule?"

Hale eyed me, then grabbed more of the food from the table, and stepped close to me.

"Eat, and I will tell you more."

I did not hesitate even slightly this time. I licked up a bite of the cakey substance and chewed. It didn't taste so strange now. In fact, my stomach seemed to rejoice as I swallowed.

"Humans must not know of the Midaworld. The way we do things doesn't match," she explained, "fear and terror yes, they would be afraid. But more...they would wish to quell our fire. Domesticate us. Make us like humans."

I licked my lips. "Like humans?" I took another bite.

"Humans must be calm, must hold in their desires and emotions. You work and slave your lives away," she growled, "no passion, no fire. So many constraints. They would hold us to them or attempt to hunt us."

I couldn't help but laugh weakly. "You're the hunter," I replied, "...we don't like being hunted and killed. You eat us."

"It is our nature," Hale told me.

"It doesn't seem like a fair fight," I said. Her hand was empty.

Hale rumbled low and crouched down closer to me. I looked into her face, examining the strange but familiar features.

"It's not," she said, "and it will never be. It's why our two worlds are two and not one."

To my surprise, she reached her claws out and cut the ropes that were holding me to the chair. I found myself looking in amazement at how her claws could be gentle enough to feed me one moment and sharp enough to cut through the rope the next.

"You have rules too," I remarked.

"Few," she replied, "...and most are about humans."

"Like...killing me for knowing," I whispered.

She looked into my face for a long moment. I wiggled my wrists and legs, wishing to stretch more, but did not.

"Little One," she purred. The vibration made my skin tingle. "I do not have to kill you, if I keep you."

My breath caught in my throat. "W-What?" I whispered.

"I want to keep you," she told me, her eyes burned brighter.

My entire body was so hot that it was excruciating. I could feel every single inch of my body prickling with goosebumps and I wanted so badly to lean in. To taste her mouth and tongue again. I could still remember the taste and feel of her lips, and her tongue invading my mouth, forcing me to eat.

I had no idea what her keeping me would entail. This large and overwhelming place around me, and a world that I did not belong in. But I found myself aching to know.

Despite this, a word hitched up from my throat. "N-No," I choked. "You can't."

Hale's gaze grew darker, and she pulled away from me.

"I need to go back," I insisted. My head was so dizzy, and panic was creeping up my spine, making my fingers twitch and palms sweat.

"Why?" she asked. "Tell me, is your life good?" She tilted her head. "Why were you in the street in the dark, screaming and crying so furiously?"

I thought perhaps she was being cruel, but her feline expression showed a sense of genuine wonder.

Cautiously, I slid my butt forward in the chair and watched for her reaction. She moved closer but did not stop me as I slid off the chair. My feet slapped against the floor as I dropped about a foot below. I kept my eyes on her as I stepped to the side. I folded my arms under my bust. Though my legs still felt a bit wobbly and weak, I needed to stretch them after being constrained.

"Don't test me," Hale spoke from behind me. My back was turned to her. "Unless you desire another chase? I can't promise I'll be able to stop."

A shiver ran up my back. I cleared my throat and closed my eyes, deciding not to reply to that.

"My life isn't good," I told her, "but not any better or worse than anyone else, I guess."

I opened my eyes and looked at the weaved brick flooring underneath my bare feet. The floor felt colder than the room where I had been kept before. "That's a lie. It sucks. It could be worse, yeah, but it's definitely not as good as it could be."

"Tell me why," Hale insists.

I turn to look at her, but not her face. My gaze was on her stomach so that I don't have to crane my neck. "My mom's dead," I explain, "my father is marrying a woman younger than me, which wouldn't be such a big deal if it seemed like he still cared about his family, about me, anymore." I shook my head. "I work a dead-end job for just enough money to survive, but I mean, who doesn't?"

I wipe my hand over my face. "There's so many little things too. It all piles up and up. Bills, politics, jerks on the street, my apartment falling apart, the rent doubling...the sun, it gives me migraines." I vented until my face was red and my head was dizzy.

"Why were you outside in the rain?" Hale asked. She seemed to follow my movements like a shadow. When I stepped farther away, she was close behind, when I moved left, she moved. Each step of mine prompted an inch of her own.

My heart ached just to think about it. I swallowed and closed my eyes again as I spoke about it.

"My boyfriend of four years dumped me on my birthday," I told her, "...for my best friend." My eyes burned. "My best friend of ten years. I have no idea how fucking long they were going on behind my back either, but God." I curled my hands into fists. "I don't know what hurts more. Her or him. I loved them both. I thought I was going to marry him, she was going to be my maid of honor."

I inhaled slowly, trying to hold back the tears, but they poured out anyway and dripped down my cheeks.

I could feel Hale up close to me, the heat...it was staggering. My knees felt weak.

"You hurt," she said, "it's so vulnerable. So strong."

My stomach was tied in knots, but I opened my eyes to look at her again.

"Tell me, Little One, if your life hurts you so much, what do you have to go back for?" she asked.

I sniffled. "Fern," I explained. "My cat. She's the one good thing in my life."

This time I tilted my head up to look into Hale's face as best I could. She leaned down more. There was a glimmer of something strange in her eyes. An emotion I hadn't seen in this monster before.

"Fern?" she repeated.

"She needs someone to take care of her. Without me

she'll...just..." I shook my head. I didn't want to think about what would happen to her, but I couldn't deny it. "Hale, she'll die. I know what you are. I know you have to kill me, or keep me, or whatever." My breath caught in my throat. "...but please. I won't tell anyone. I promise."

More tears dripped down my face.

Hale crouched down and brushed one of her claws along my cheek, collecting the salty tears.

"I can't...just leave her," I insisted. I felt so desperate. Knowing I needed to be there for Fern, and aching in the presence of Hale at the same time. I leaned on my legs, struggling to stay standing. Whatever strength I had was dwindling again.

"You should rest," Hale said. Her voice was low.

I shook my head. "No."

Suddenly, her muscular arms were underneath me, legs and back, and I was lifted from the floor. "Please," I said. I didn't understand why she even cared about my resting. Why she wanted to know about my life? What happened to me was entirely up to her.

Hale started out of the room with me.

"You *will* rest," she said.

And much like anything else, I could not fight her on that.

5

FREE BIRD

Renee

Hale had laid me down in what I could only describe as a nest. Bundles of fabric, blankets, and pillows all piled up in the corner of a dimly lit room. I wasn't entirely certain if there was a mattress, but it was fairly soft and comfortable, anyway. I was still warmer than I was used to, so I didn't cover up with anything. I wasn't sure how long I was lying there, nor how long I had been sleeping; but before I had fallen asleep, I had simply cried.

I didn't care if she was there watching me or feeding off my sadness. I felt overwhelmed. I missed Fern and I was worried about her. Monsters existed. A whole other realm existed. Processing this was a lot. I wasn't sure how long I'd even have to process.

Would Hale keep me there like she wanted, or would I die?

These thoughts followed me into my sleep, where darkness invaded, as did the large hands of my captor. In my dreams, Hale touched every inch of me and my body responded in pleasure. Her long tongue delved deep within me and my hips rocked needily against each thrust and lick. I knew it was a dream, and I fought to stay in it as long as possible.

But it was shorter lived than I wanted.

Light shined through my eyelids and forced them to crack open.

The sun poured into my vision and I closed my eyes, my head already aching. I tossed an arm over my face and debated falling back asleep. Then it hit me.

The sun?

I had seen no hint of the yellow blinding sun in the Midaworld until now. Only a strange red glow. Not the light of the sun I was used to.

I quickly opened my eyes and sat up. My hands at my sides. My fingers gripped the ground beneath me. Not blankets or pillows, no, but grass.

My vision cleared, and I could see where I was.

A field, surrounded by trees on all sides. The sun was near the middle of the clear blue sky.

My pulse quickened, and I looked around me for any sign of anyone else. Hale. I saw nothing but trees, grass, and small purple and white flowers barely taller than the blades.

"She let me go?" I whispered.

As my head cleared, it was the only thing that made sense. Why? I didn't know. Maybe there was some...weird feline connection there. Hearing about Fern had broken through? I shook my head.

No. I don't know.

I took a deep breath of fresh air, then again. It felt good. I slowly pushed up from the ground and onto my feet. I felt tired, but stronger. As I debated which direction to go in the field, I questioned things.

Was Hale even real?

I looked down. I was still in the long cream-colored dress. Where else would I have gotten it? How would I have gotten here on my own?

It was too much to go through. My stomach growled and pulled me back to the present. I needed to get out of the woods, or wherever I was.

I decide to follow the direction of the sun. As I pushed through some brush, I heard cars. I was near a road. I continued through the trees, wincing as twigs and pine needles poked at my feet, but they didn't slow me down. I needed to get home.

It wasn't long before I reached the road. It was only a quarter mile if that from the clearing. I stood at the edge of the trees and looked out at the road about two yards away. Cars were whizzing passed with only a few glances in my direction as I walked along the side of the road on the grass. My eyes darted around and looked for any sign of where I was.

"This is what we get for relying on Google Maps." I sighed.

But I was lucky enough to spot a bus stop with a map and make out just how far away I was from the bus stop near my apartment building. There was an older man sitting on the bench.

"Are you alright?" he asked me as I looked at the worn plastic map fixed to the glass.

"Yes, thank you," I replied and kept my back turned, feeling anxious about being alone with him.

Then blinked and smiled to myself. I was anxious about being alone with a man? I was just kidnapped by a literal monster! I put a hand to my mouth and kept from laughing, but my stomach clenched.

I took a deep breath composed myself before looking at the map again.

"Fifteen miles," I calculated, "damn."

It wasn't exactly an easy walk, but...hell, I could have been left in another country. So I was grateful I was even nearby.

I turned and looked as a bus pulled up and the man got up to get on. I chewed on the inside of my cheek, thinking. I didn't have my phone or purse, no way to pay to ride the bus. I looked on the ground and spotted a quarter and some other change. I scooped it up and shuffled toward the bus. It definitely wasn't going to be enough, it but was something.

I got on just before the doors were closing.

"I don't have much, but I really need to get home," I explained and held my hand out. The look on the bus driver's face was unamused. I was prepared for him to tell me to get off. With my luck, I'd be walking the entire fifteen miles home.

But he hummed and counted the change in my hand.

"You're eighteen," he said, and motioned to the chart.

There was a reduced rate for those 18 and under fifty cents.

I blinked. "Uh, yeah," I went along.

I nodded and put the change into the meter. "Have a seat." He didn't ask for ID or anything, and waited for me to sit down nearby.

I exhaled in relief once the bus was moving. He looked at me with concern once or twice at the nearest stop light.

"Everything okay, young lady?" he asked, "...you shouldn't be out with no shoes."

I brushed my wild curls behind my ears. I had no idea how I looked, but it couldn't be good. Thin dress, no shoes, messy hair and face.

"Y-Yeah," I lied. "I just want to get home."

He eyed me and went back to driving safely. There were some other eyes on me and whispers, but I ignored them.

People got on and off the bus, and I just paid attention to the feeling of the road underneath the tires. I helped distract my mind. The closer I got to the stop I needed, the more eager to make sure Fern was okay I got.

Finally, it was my stop.

"Hey," the driver said as I was walking up. "You call this number. You need any help, right?"

I took the card he had in his fingers and nodded. "Thanks," I smiled weakly.

I got off the bus and back into the bright sun. I looked down at the card. It had the address and number for a women's shelter. I smiled a little more now and looked back at the bus before it pulled off.

Sometimes people weren't as bad as it felt like.

The pavement was warm as I walked. I was two miles from my building. I knew the way from here, and I knew the shortest way. But the safest way was the longest. I avoided sharp objects on the sidewalk as best I could and kept my eyes away from others. I didn't want to answer questions about my state and I definitely didn't want to pay any hecklers attention. It wasn't so bad in the middle of the day, and it must have been a weekday because there was fewer people out.

Which meant I had definitely been gone a couple days. My heart sank.

"I hope Fern is okay."

I walked faster, even though it hurt my feet. The closer I got, the more energy I had.

Finally, I was at my building. I rushed up to the second floor, trying not to trip over the dress, and made it to my door. It was then that I realized I had no idea how I was going to get in; but something dangled from the door handle. My purse!

I grabbed it and quickly looked inside.

My ID was still inside, along with other cards, my phone, but my money and emergency snacks were gone. Of course...but fuck, they'd at least brought it to my address!

"Keys!" I grabbed them from the side pocket. Before I could even get the door unlocked, I heard scratching and yowling from the other side of the door.

"Oh, Fern, mama's coming," I whispered and unlocked the door.

I opened the door and tossed my purse inside. Fern, in all of her fluffy gray glory, leaped at me and placed her paws on my chest as I dropped to the floor.

"Fern! Baby...I'm so sorry," I cried, "...I don't even know how to explain it to you...but oh hell, I'm here now." I wrapped her up in my arms and cuddled her so tightly. She licked my face and nose and nuzzled into me frantically, meowing.

"Okay, it's okay," I assured her.

I stood up with her in my arms and used my foot to close the door.

"You're so hungry, I know," I whispered. "Thank god I got that water fountain."

At least she wasn't thirsty when I was gone.

"Oh, sweet baby, such a good girl." I scratched her ears and bounced her in one arm as I grabbed a scoop of food and put it in her bowl, along with several treats.

"Go on, eat some food." I tried to set her down, but she didn't want to go. I grabbed some food in my hand and let her eat from my hand.

Doing this reminded me of Hale, and I couldn't help but laugh. How strange it was to look at Fern after seeing Hale. Hale was feline, but distinctly different from the feline I was holding in my arms now. One a monster, the other a pet.

Fern finally let me put her down so she could eat her food and I sighed, simply watching her eat for a long moment.

The shower called out to me, and I stripped off the strange garment and enjoyed the hot water. It soothed the ache in my joints and muscles, as well as the headache that was coming on. Still, even as I relaxed, I couldn't help but think about Hale.

Maybe I'd just gotten really drunk after what happened on my birthday and completely blacked out. That seemed like it would make the most sense compared to a monster kidnapping me...

But the proof was there. The dress she had put me in. The slight bruises and marks along my body from the ropes. Even the scab on my bottom lip from where she had nipped me with her sharp teeth.

I wanted to believe in her, but I also didn't. It was easier to think that it had all been my imagination. So much easier than admitting that I had enjoyed being chased and desired by such a creature.

Once I was dried off and wrapped in a robe, I checked on Fern. She was curled up on the floor near the end of my bed on the dress I had taken off, sniffing it and nuzzling into it.

My heart bloomed knowing she was okay.

Despite my desire to cuddle her and never let go, I made some food and sat on my bed in my studio apartment, eating it, and avoiding my memories. It wasn't easy.

After my phone was charged, I checked my social media. It had been two and a half days. I wasn't sure if it felt longer or shorter. Nor how time even worked in the...Midaworld. If that was where I had been.

No one had questioned where I was. There were some messages, but all were casual. A post on Casey's Facebook page. My jaw tightened. It was a picture of her and Kevin out for lunch. He had his arm around her and she was kissing his cheek. It was an announcement of their relationship. Their first "public" date.

"Fucking bitch," I snarled. Since my birthday, neither of them had even messaged me to check on me. No calls either.

"How is someone my best friend for ten years, and...doesn't even...care how I am?" I whispered. Maybe I should have seen it coming. She'd been growing more distant and busy the last couple years. I thought it was her new job and her boyfriend. Certainly not my boyfriend.

"Who cares..." I flopped onto my back. My plate was empty. "If they want to be assholes together, fine. I'm good."

I wasn't good. Not at all. But after the last couple days, it didn't seem to matter as much. Fern climbed up onto the bed and laid on my stomach to make biscuits against me. I smiled softly at her and just watched before checking my texts.

Three texts from my boss. All annoyed at me for not being at work, but none asking if I was okay. No genuine concern, just warnings. My eyes burned. Did no one in my life really care about me?

Well, at least my grandma had sent me a birthday card. A week early, but there was that. She was the only person who seemed to care, but she struggled to remember who I was or who she was those days.

I looked back down at Fern and pet her gently. "You really are the good thing in my life," I told her. "Such a sweet girl." She bonked her face against the back of my hand, signaling that she wanted me to pet her head specifically. "Yeah," I cooed, "yes you are."

Fern made me feel calm and comfortable. It was easier to forget about the people who seemed to already forget me when I was cuddling and petting her.

Still, thoughts of Hale plagued me throughout the day of relaxing and taking care of myself. Her glowing red eyes and how they seared me with each look.

Her words of desiring me. Her purrs and growls. The way she towered above me with her broad shoulders and thick curves. Her powerful arms underneath me.

I shivered and closed my eyes. "We just need to sleep." I took my robe off and pulled the blanket onto myself. It was dark out now. I found I had to turn the AC up, when usually I had to turn it down. Had I gotten used to the warmer temperature so easily?

I shook the thought out of my head. I needed to think about something else.

Hale was gone. I was home. I wouldn't tell anyone about her, if it was even real. And I needed to never think about it again.

Easy.

Done.

One hundred percent.

Who's Hale?

Nope.

Not thinking about it.

Her nose pressed near my pussy. Her hot breath. The pure adrenaline as she chased me. The look in her eyes as I spoke of my life and of Fern.

The fact that she had fed me and let me rest. She had let me go, despite the rules. She had left me in a field near the road and let me live.

Her craving for my life and my body... I squeezed my thighs together, feeling hot and eager now.

I squirmed in my bed, feeling more restless as the night went on so slowly.

I sat up, panting softly. I couldn't deny it. I wanted her. I wanted the thrill, the chase, the passion. I had never felt so real and unchained as I had than I was with her. Despite the bindings, despite the kidnapping. It had all felt so freeing in a way I didn't understand.

Every part of me ached for more. Ached to be near her again. To be chased and taken by her. To be held by her. To hear her low raspy voice and feel her claws against my flesh.

"Fuck this," I hissed.

What was my life? The same boring and stressful thing day after day, broken up by pain and the occasional positive... I had felt more at place in a world that wasn't my own than I did in this one.

I didn't want to die, no; I wanted to be somewhere else. I wanted to be with Hale. I needed her. I wasn't sure she needed me, but it didn't matter.

I pulled myself out of bed and got dressed in that damn long dress again. It was more comfortable than anything I owned. I slipped on some shoes as well.

"Okay Fern, come on," I coaxed her into her carrier, placing her favorite toys and some food in it. "mama's getting us out of here." I knew the bus stop I'd started at earlier in the day. I could take a bus back there. Maybe...I'd be able to find her. Get her attention, somehow. I had no idea how it worked, but... I couldn't lay there in bed in my cruddy apartment anymore.

There was a chance I was losing my mind. I realized that.

It didn't stop me.

6

THE ONE WITH THE MATING

Hale

I stalked the night like the predator I am. Searching for something, someone, to quench the perverse thirst I felt. I was so hungry that it hurt, and I could sense all the emotion around me. None of it was as strong as Renee. The purity of her raw emotions was like a high I was had ridden on and clung to until it was all gone. Until she was gone.

The memory of her anger, fear, and lust was still fresh, but nothing compared to being up close to it. Feeling it soak into every inch of me without me even attempting to drink it in.

Even as I hid in the shadows and decided on my prey, I thought of her. I thought of her sweet lips and the curves of her body so delicate and round. I could break her with a snap of my fingers, but breaking her was the last thing I wanted to do to her.

Just the thought of Renee grew the desire and hunger inside me. Yet I had let her go.

I had killed with no thought for the human life. I was tempted many times, but killing her... I could not bear the thought. I could not have her, and I could not kill her.

I growled in the darkness and disappeared behind street lamps in quick shadowed movements as I chased the drunken businessman, completely unaware of just how much danger he was in.

Frustration rolled off him as he muttered to himself, taking drags of a smoke every now and again. The closer I got, the more desperate I grew to take every drop of that emotion and soul. I listened to his pulse and counted each of his steps as he drew closer to the alleyway. His intoxicated swagger was slower than I'd like.

The patience I might have had before had dwindled to nothing in just the hours without Renee.

He was number five, and I was still...so...hungry.

Faster than any human could process, I pulled him into the alley and slammed him against a wall. His breath washed out of him as I held his feet above the ground like he was nothing. He was.

The horror of my piercing face and glistening teeth reflected in his eyes, and it delighted me. He couldn't make a noise, paralyzed by fear that I hoped would feed me well. Urine dripped down his pant leg.

My eyes grew brighter as I took in that feeling. Terror, confusion, and disbelief. It flowed from him in a colorful transparent haze, flooding into my eyes and mouth and becoming one with me. As I took more and more from him, his face grew placid and pale. If I stopped, he could live. He would be hung over for quite some time, feel...empty for a while; but he would recover, soul intact.

I didn't stop.

I gorged myself on him, taking until he was nothing but an empty husk. His emaciated body fell limp to the asphalt. His pulse and breath left him, and he was gone.

I shivered as his energy intertwined with mine. Every second of his life flashed through my mind. Every moment of suffering, joy, lust, and calm. Then, it was gone, all in a moment.

It wasn't enough. I felt as though I was starving in a desert full of ripe fruit that no longer sated me.

"Fuck!" I growled. I slammed my fist into the brick wall, smashing chunks of it into grit that sprinkled onto the ground and blew away in the wind. As lights flickered on, I disappeared into the night once more.

How many would I go through to fill myself? How long would I go chasing the cure for the ache?

Just as the night felt as though it may drive me to the point of insanity far beyond even a monster, I felt it.

That same ripple of emotion that broke through to me several nights before. Like an earthquake sending waves of motion even miles away. Hot and burning through me like nothing before.

Renee. It was her. It had to be.

Was something wrong?

I fought the urge to follow the barrage of emotions that were hitting me, telling myself I could not see her again. I had let her go.

"Hale!"

I heard it as if it was right next to me, no, within me. A call so strong that it shook me to my core. I squeezed my eyes shut and rumbled in frustration as I tried to ignore it.

Every part of me lit up as I felt Renee's desperate emotion flood me, and her voice call out for me again. It was an experience I had heard of, but never felt before.

I couldn't resist, and I could not stop myself from following the rush of emotion and need that called out to me. Crossing roads and rivers, I rushed by trees and houses in the night.

The complete and utter passion that roared out to me and sur-rounded me, lulled me closer and closer, could only be one thing. I wasn't ready to admit it, even as I followed it.

As I grew closer, my hunger grew ten fold and knotted me from the inside out. I realized I was back where I had left Renee. In a field near a road, close enough that she could find her way out, but I would not be seen whilst carrying her.

Her scent hit me as I stepped out from the trees. She stood there in the same dress I had given her, but the tresses of her light brown hair were in soft, clean ringlets, and her face was red and dripping with tears, her eyes flooded by frustration.

A growl erupted from my chest as I glared at her from across the grass.

"What the fuck are you doing?" I asked, voice low, but I knew she could hear it.

Those tear-filled eyes suddenly lit up, and she whirled around, running from me.

I didn't hesitate, following behind her, my teeth bared and fur bristled. I listened as her blood pumped harder and her breath grew quick and shallow.

"Why are you doing this?" I huffed from behind her.

She turned quickly, not diving into the trees but simply going in a circle around in the field. Her feet stamped against the grass, but mine left scorched earth in their path.

I reached out, grabbed her from behind, and turned her around. My claws tore the fabric and nicked her skin. I could smell even the barest drop of her sweet blood. A moan rumbled out, and I pushed her against a tree, holding her above the ground, my grip on her tight.

Renee whined out at me and squirmed, but she was not trying to get away from me.

"What is this?" I growled, my mouth near her ear.

Renee sucked in a breath and looked into my face. I could smell her arousal... wet and decadent between her thighs. Her blood flushing her thighs hotter than anywhere else. I responded to her in kind and pressed closer to her.

"Why are you here?" I asked. "Answer me!" I demanded. My eyes flared brighter and reflected against her face.

"I want you!" Renee choked out. "I need you."

My eyes widened, and my hands tightened against her.

"I want you to chase me, take me... I can't handle my life, as it is," she told me, her hands coming to grip at my shoulders, curling into my fur and against my skin. I shivered at her cooler touch.

"You don't know what you're saying," I squeezed my eyes shut. If I didn't, I wasn't sure what I might do.

"Yes, I do!" she spat out at me. "I want the rush, the...passion, I want you." Her hands slid up to my face. "Look at me, please!" She begged, and I could not deny her. I looked into her burning eyes with my own.

"I want you, Hale, even if it's wrong. Even if means giving up everything I know. My entire life for a new one." Her breath hitched in her throat, but her words were strong and clear.

"Renee," I purred and tried to look away, but her hands coaxed me out of it. Her fingers pressed into my hot flesh, her thumbs caressing my cheeks.

"I could devour you," I warned her.

"Take me, devour me, let me be yours," Renee begged.

That haze of her emotion surrounded me, flowing from her in orange and red hues that sparkled in the moonlight. As I breathed in, it filled my mouth and eyes. Just a sip filled me more than any of the others had.

I could feel her absolute devotion invade me.

The darkness that created me called for me to take as much as I could, to take all of her, but I stopped myself. Letting the haze recede back within her beautiful face.

The ache within dulled for now.

"Little One," I hummed.

"Please," Renee crooned.

Once again, I could not deny her. I ran my tongue along the curve of her neck, tasting the salty sweat that gathered there. She shivered in response, and the fire burned hotter within.

I held her steady against the sturdy tree and slowly lowered myself. My hands slid to the crook of her knees and I slipped her legs over my shoulders. I felt her hands slide to my head, fingers curling around the small horns that jutted out a few inches back from my forehead. No one had touched them in quite some time. Her hands were chilly and her pulse strong. I groaned at the tingle that lit me up and quickly moved the skirt of her dress up.

My head buried between her plump thighs, I ran my nose along the seam of her panties, feeling the dampness there. The scent of her arousal took over my every sense and heated my body to an extreme that I could hardly control.

I growled against her flesh. Renee's breath hitched in her throat as I ran my tongue along her clothed pussy. I was desperate to please her.

My sharp nails pressed against her thighs, and they squeezed against my head.

"Hale," she said in a breath. "Please, I need you."

Those words were all I needed to prompt me to rip her panties from her body, the fabric nothing but shreds in the grass below.

I licked at her wet lips, the tip of my tongue grazing her entrance. I could feel how hot and ready she was. Her hips quivered against my face and her hands squeezed my horns so perfectly. I gripped her tighter as I slipped my long tongue inside of her velvety cunt one inch at a time. I lapped her juices and swirled at her precious sweet spot as she ground against me, moaning and squirming.

"Oh, oh God," Renee panted. Her body struggled to stay rigid against the tree, so I held her even tighter.

I pulled my tongue from her dripping cunt. "I got you," I purred. I licked again, twirling the tips of my tongue against her swollen clit. "Fuck, you're so wet for me." My tail flicked up from behind me and wrapped around her body until the pointed end rubbed against her breasts.

"M-More, please, don't stop." She moved her hips toward my mouth desperately.

It overwhelmed me with desire, hers and my own. It surrounded us like a pink and orange fog that blinded me from everything but her. My own wet arousal dripped between my thighs, soaking me entirely.

She was all I saw, smelled, felt, and all I needed.

7

INTENSITY

Renee

My entire body was a live wire. I was hot from head to toe and I wanted more and more. As Hale's tongue filled me again, fuller than anyone ever had before, the pressure within my groin and abdomen grew stronger. It shivered down my thighs that had captured her head and bubbled up all the way to my belly button.

"Yes, oh, fuck, fuck, fuck me!" I cried. I rocked my hips quick and rough against her face, thrusting her tongue in and out of me even more. Her tail caressed my hard nipple through the fabric and sent electric through my nerves.

My breath grew quicker, my voice more desperate and thoughts erratic as I was overcome by my orgasm. My entire body shivered and tensed as I came, but she did not stop. Hale continued to fuck me with her tongue even as I cried out in ecstasy and slapped my hand over my mouth, trying not to be too loud.

The pleasure was stronger than I had ever felt. It flushed me so brilliantly pink and pulsed in my pussy and thighs so hard that I wasn't sure when it ended.

I yelped softly against my palm as her tongue emptied me and my cum gushed from my hole onto her chest, glistening at her collarbones.

"Do not quiet yourself, Little One," she growled. "You are mine, and I will hear you."

I moaned in response as my dizzy head would not allow me words.

Suddenly, I was lifted away from the tree and lowered to the ground. My back hit the grass, which tickled at first and I couldn't help but giggle breathlessly.

Hale's hands and claws slid my dress up over my head, and I lifted my arms to allow her. Though I knew she could so easily rip it off like my panties had been.

For a moment, my eyes darted to where I had left Fern's carrier, and I saw she was still inside, curled up and nuzzling one of her toys. Knowing she was okay, I let the thought of her leave my mind as I was left bare to the open air and Hale's glowing red eyes.

Those eyes scanned over me in lust and desire, but there was also something else there. A passion so pure and devotion so true that I was certain it could never come from any of the humans I had dated in my past.

I squeezed my thighs together as I caught my breath, but it was taken from me as I watched Hale stand above me, a couple feet to the side, and remove her clothing. Though minimal, her clothing fell to the ground, and her large, soft breasts with dark red areola and hard nipples came into view. My eyes followed the lines of her muscular yet soft body.

"Wow," I whispered. Feeling as though there may as well have been stars in my eyes.

I could not believe it was happening, but it was, and I was going to cherish it in my memories forever. However long forever was.

My gaze finally landed on her groin, and what I saw there both comforted and surprised me. Between her strong soft things was a wet and needy pussy, bigger than my own as her entire person was. It made my arousal shiver up my spine. Above that, however, near the top of her lips was a clit much larger than I was used to. It was partially hooded and angled downward, but protruded a couple inches longer than mine and was wider. Though it differed from my own, I knew what I was looking at, but I was uncertain of its exact function in comparison. My cunt pulsed between my closed thighs.

My breath caught in my throat as I looked.

"Is everything to your liking?" she asked me.

I licked my lips and nodded. "Yes," I replied, "very much."

She stepped closer, and I could see her even better as we were bathed in moonlight. Her enlarged clit didn't appear to have a slit of any kind.

"Are you curious?" Hale asked as she lowered herself to the ground.

My face flushed deeper. "My mate," she whispered as she leaned in and pressed her fingers to my cheek. "You are my mate," she repeated, "I feel it in my bones."

Though I did not entirely understand what she meant, my heart swelled, and I leaned up even closer to her.

"...I'm drawn to you unlike any other," Hale crooned and licked at my lips. I could taste my arousal on my own lips now.

I exhaled a shaky breath. "I'm yours," I whispered and leaned in. I kissed her, soft but ardent. Tasting even more of myself and enjoying every bit. Our lips melted together so perfectly, the heat of her body extreme in the best way.

I pulled away and looked down her body once more. Hale leaned back and sat back on the grass, spreading her long legs and baring herself to me.

"Explore," she husked, "all you want. All you need. I am yours."

I sat up completely and crawled over to her and between her legs. I could see the wetness there, dripping and hot. My arms were shaky, but I didn't want to stop. I needed more. She watched me as she leaned back on her arms, her eyes burning with the need and hunger that I mirrored.

I lowered myself between her thighs and licked the tip of her clit. Seeing it up close, the familiar hood and taste of her juices. I drew her clitoral hood up with two of my fingers and explored the short sensitive length with my tongue, getting a feel for it.

Hale moaned, and her hips jerked at my touch. Though my tongue was much smaller and limited in movement than hers, it was no less talented in making her breath hitch and her pussy throb; it seemed.

It grew familiar quickly. Taking her swollen clit in my mouth where it fit perfectly, hitting just at the center of my tongue.

"Ah-Ah, fuck..." Hale rocked against my face.

My hands moved to her thighs, pressing against them and holding them apart as well as I could, but she was strong.

I flicked my tongue along her clit quickly in expert strokes. My only desire at that moment was to make her feel as good as I did. Hale's swollen clit throbbed against my tongue. My pussy ached at the taste of her, musky and delicious.

I ran my hands along her thighs, feeling her hot skin broken up by patches of soft fur under my fingers. As I looked up at her from my place between her thighs and saw her head tilted back, her sharp teeth bared as she moaned, I was even more turned on. Her hands palmed her own breasts and tweaked her nipples.

I gave her pussy two more long licks before I moved up because I couldn't resist myself.

I sat straddling her lap and hips as best as I could and pressed my cunt down against hers. Her clit was such a perfect size for grinding against and her pussy, so wet and warm.

Hale slid back off her arms and laid completely down. I placed my hands on her stomach as I rocked my hips against her.

"Yes, oh...fuck," I panted, and she met my moans with her own.

"Oh, Little One, fuck you're so wet, you're so good..." she growled out, her hips bucking up against me. I felt her hand smack hard against one of my ass cheeks, leaving it stinging and hot.

Our movements grew more frantic and needy. Sweat dripped down my body and onto hers, our scents mingling to create the perfect provocative perfume.

"Yes, oh...Hale," I cried out, tossing my head back and letting my curls graze her thighs behind me.

I dripped with arousal and shivered in ecstasy. In this moment, I was in control of the monster who shivered and rocked underneath me. Knowing this made me practically glow with pleasure.

Her clit pressed to my entrance with each rock of my hips, just barely pressing inside. I shifted my hips more and gasped softly as I felt it slip inside me deeper. Shallow, but electrifying.

Hale's hands gripped me tightly, and her claws pressed into my thighs, stinging and sinking in deeper. I cried out as I felt the blood drip down my flesh and the sharpness grew into a burning pain. It only spurred me on, and my entire body quivered as I came.

"Good girl," Hale husked and pushed her pussy and clit harder up against me. "Ah-Ah!" She went rigid as she came and I felt her clit throbbing inside of me, her pussy pulsing against me, and her juices soaked me and the grass even further.

All of my breath was gone from me, and I leaned forward with my hair in front of my face and brushing against her breasts. My hips twitched as the pleasure continued to tingle up and down my thighs. I could hardly hold myself up with my arms anymore.

Hale purred underneath me, her hips still rocking against me, slow and steady.

"More," she growled.

I hummed out dizzily. "I can't..." I licked my lips. And looked through my hair at her face. Her eyes were burning even brighter.

All in a split second, I was on my back again and she was between my thighs, spreading them wider and sinking even deeper against me. My breath caught in my throat and my arms laid at the sides of my head. Hale's night dark hair fell all around my head and brushed my shoulders and chest before disappearing as she stretched out more. Her breasts at my face. I moved my head and face just enough to take one of her nipples into my mouth and lick it in slow circles. The nub hardened even more in my wet mouth.

My slow movements were quickly interrupted as Hale's clit slipped back inside of me those couple inches and she began to thrust and grind against me, quick and hard.

Heat rushed up my spine so fast it made my vision blurry.

"Hale!" I choked out. My hands gripped onto the grass as best as possible, but it just ripped out of the ground.

Hale's body went rigid and her muscles harder than before, but her hips kept moving, contorting her body with each rough thrust that smacked against the inside of my thighs.

My moans and breaths became indistinguishable between the sounds of Hale's growling and grunting.

I could hear the ground above my head being ripped apart, dirt and roots displaced.

I squeezed my eyes shut as I felt another orgasm ripping through my tired, overstimulated body. Somehow, I loved it. The rush that overtook me and burned me through from head to toe was exhilarating. My thighs and hips twitched and quivered as I laid there, body going limp. I felt like Jell-O.

Hale panted and shivered hard against me as her body relaxed. She relaxed down against me, heavy and hot, but didn't put all her weight on me.

"Mistress," I whispered, dizzily. The word seemed to just escape me so naturally. I was too exhausted to be embarrassed.

Hale pulled her groin from mine and slid down until her face was above mine and our hair mingled together.

"Little One," Hale husked and nuzzled her face into my neck and shoulder. At that moment, I didn't have one care or thought about the pathetic man who had broken my heart only days before.

A light breeze washed over us, collecting my sweat and cooling me off as I laid there.

If we could, I'd be happy to stay there until the sun rose.

8

AVOIDANCE

Hale

Basking in the afterglow. Warm. Full. Surrounded by the calm, sensual emotion that radiated off Renee and intertwined with my own. Every inch of me was sweaty, and so was every inch of her.

After *Chesa* knew how long of laying on the ground, I moved up and off Renee. She was asleep, her breath shallow. I looked at her nude body in the grass. Above and around her, the ground was tattered and torn, with dirt strewn all over.

The moon was still bright in the sky. Renee looked beautiful in the light. Her body is so soft. My eyes caught the shallow puncture wounds on the sides of her thighs, and heat built up within me again. I could imagine the taste of her blood. My tongue ran along my teeth.

She was too tired now. If I was to drink her blood, I wanted her wide awake and begging.

I wondered if she would regret my marks on her body, or if she would desire them. She was a strange human who threw my expectations off. I grinned widely and stood to my full height.

I needed to get us out of there before the sun rose. It was unlikely that anyone would see. But I wasn't going to take the chance. I looked over at the carrier with the meowing creature right as Renee stirred from her sleep.

A cat. Her cat. Fern. Renee had claimed that this Fern was the one good thing in her life. How deeply she cared for the animal—one more pure than me—had struck a strange cord in me. A cord of humanity.

"It wasn't a dream," Renee mumbled from her place on the ground. Her hair was splayed out in wild tangles that crowned her head.

I tilted my head and met her gaze from above. My body cast a shadow over her entirely.

"No," I replied, "or I would never wake." I pulled and secured my clothing in place.

I crouched down to be closer to her. "We must leave now." The scent of her arousal and skin found me. If we did not leave, I would not be able to resist making her cry out into the early morning.

Renee sighed and sat up. I stood and held out a hand for her. Her delicate fingers wrapped around two of my own and she pulled herself from the ground. She swayed on her feet; I moved to sweep her off them.

"Wait!" she insisted. She took several steps forward and grabbed the carrier off the ground, holding it in both of her arms. "Alright."

I took her naked form into my arms, her legs dangling over one of them. Renee was quiet. She rested her head against my chest and simply looked up at me. I could hear Fern complaining, and saw her small white claws poke out of the netted front.

"It's okay, you'll get out soon I promise," Renee cooed to the creature. Her voice was higher and softer.

Something stirred inside me. I brushed it away.

The clearing disappeared as the mortal realm melted into the Midaworld. For a moment we were between realms, but as quickly as a blink, I stood in the doorway of my familiar dwelling. I paid no mind to the surroundings, as I had one room in mind. In just a few footfalls, I turned into the bathroom. A large claw foot bath rest in the middle of the room, the centerpiece. Vintage, perhaps, for the human idea of time. Well taken care of.

"A bath?" Renee said, her voice full of relief. "Thank goodness."

A crooked grin tugged at one corner of my mouth.

I set Renee down gently, despite enjoying her in my arms.

I watched as she set the carrier down and unzipped it.

Fern, a small furry cat that looked so small compared to me was disconcerting, slowly stepped out. She turned her snout up and looked at me. A look of judgment and confusion crossed her face.

"It's alright Fern, this is Hale. She won't hurt you." Renee looked over and up at me. "Right?" Her brow furrowed slightly. She leaned down and stroked the kitten's head.

I tilted my head. I'd never much cared for human pets. Much less the ones that could very well be long ago ancestors. There was something unnerving about standing face to face with a creature I shared similarities to, but they were a harmless pet; and I was not.

"I will not," I replied.

I watched the cat step closer and sniff my ankle and foot.

Fern seemed to have the same uncomfortable feeling as me. Which she showed by baring her teeth and hissing. Her fur stood on end and caused the fur on the back of my neck and shoulders to do the same.

I bared my teeth in return and growled low.

Fern narrowed her eyes and clamped her feet harder against the floor.

I maintained eye contact with her, feeling a tingle along my claws, and my pupils widened.

"Um," Renee stepped closer to Fern, "it's alright." Her voice held uncertainty; and I was uncertain which of us she was truly speaking to.

Fern spoke, and I understood. "Mom. Protect. I will."

I spoke back. "Safe. Promise."

We stared at each other for another long moment.

Fern's body relaxed, but she kept her eyes on me even as she pattered away to the corner of the bathroom and sat down after a few turns. Always watching.

"What was that?" Renee asked.

I looked at her, seeing her eyes were wide and laced with confusion. I relaxed now and shook my head. "She's protective of you," I said. My eyes darkened, and I moved closer. "I can relate."

Renee's face flushed, and she looked over at her pet once more before looking at the bath.

Before she could move to do anything, I went about filling it with hot water and sprinkled in a scent, deep but not overpowering.

I turned to Renee once more, looking at her naked body before me. I scanned her hungrily, seeing the feathered marks and bruises along her skin.

"It's a pity we left the dress behind," she commented, "I was getting used to it."

I picked her up again, and she yelped softly in surprise. "We will fashion you another," I insisted, "anything you desire."

She smiled up at me.

I placed her in the bath, starting with her toes. "Too hot?" I asked.

She hissed between her teeth, but then sighed as her body relaxed. "No, it's amazing." She tilted her head back and closed her eyes.

I let my clothing drop to the floor and slid in behind her, pulling her into my lap as the water shifted.

Renee shivered and pushed her ass firmer against my lap before relaxing. I tilted my head down and brushed my nose against her neck.

"You smell delicious," I purred, "washing the sex and dirt from you is a shame I am conflicted by." I ran my tongue along her skin, tasting the essence of her dried sweat and desire.

Renee hummed. "You'll just have to make me dirty again, and again, I guess."

I growled low and found my claws in her hair near the base of her neck. "I will so enjoy it, my mate."

My other hand brought water up over her shoulders and along her hair. She moaned softly as the water steamed from her skin. I found myself relaxed by the water, though it was only warm to me. The way she tilted her head to the side, eyes closed, waiting so needy for my touch... it was as devastatingly wonderful as the blood moon.

"What did you mean when you called me your mate?" Renee asked, "last night and now."

My hands slid around her body, and I brushed the tads of my fingers along her breasts, finding her sensitive nipples. She shivered.

"Many creatures of the Midaworld have a true mate. Your kind would call them soulmates, but to my kind, it is more than that," I told her slowly. "More than I can put to words."

Renee tensed in my grasp for a moment, before she shifted on my lap and turned herself so that she was straddling my lap, facing me.

"Try?" she asked, looking up at me, her wet hair clinging to her neck and chest.

I inhaled slowly, closing my eyes for a moment and trying to ignore the flood of hunger I felt. My tongue ran over my lips.

"I often need to feed from the emotions and souls of many, but since you... I want for nothing else. I am invigorated by your emotions, so intense and passionate. They drew us together. I want to devour you whole, and protect you all the same." My eyes were open now.

I placed my claws on her cheek and pressed lightly. Renee closed her eyes and swallowed hard. I watched her throat move and goose-bumps rise on her chest just above her breasts.

"What if I'm not?" she asked, keeping her eyes closed.

I pulled her closer and held her tighter, sloshing the water. "You are," I told her. "I am certain."

Renee opened her eyes. I shifted her in my lap so that she did not need to tilt her head so much to look into my face. "What if this doesn't work?" she asked, her voice faltering. "I was certain things with my ex would. I was wrong."

I growled softly. My hands slid down her body to her plush thighs and ran the tips of my claws along the healing wounds there. She whimpered and her hips twitched, but she did not pull away. I hated the idea of the human man who had hurt her.

"There is no leaving now," I told her, "You are mine."

Renee placed her hands on my bare chest, her fingers curling against my skin and fur tightly.

"I'm not letting go of you again," I said, my voice rough and husky.

Renee slid her hands up to my shoulders and wrapped her arms around my neck, pulling me down. "I'm yours, monster mine." Her lips were so close.

I took her mouth as mine and kissed her deeply. My tongue invaded her mouth and danced with hers. Her moans into my mouth only made me draw her closer and tighter against me until there was no space to be removed.

"Oh, Little One," I growled into her mouth. "You ignite me."

Renee stopped me from speaking any further as she deepened the kiss again, her mouth greedy and her fingers tangled in my hair.

I knew I would need to claim her eventually, truly and completely claim her. Or it would not be safe if another creature of the Midaworld were to come across her. Claiming humans had not been done for so long, as it had once posed a bigger risk. I could not imagine, however, a risk Renee could pose to the Midaworld...

Only the risk it could pose to her.

I would protect her with every flame in my flesh, so that she was mine and mine alone.

9

HUNG OVER

I'd never taken a more perfect bath in my life. Hale's hands and claws drew over me with the perfect pressure to wash away the sweat, dirt, and crusted blood from my body. And drive me wild with desire for her. In more ways than I could process at that moment. She detangled my wet curls with her claws like they were made for it.

Every second with her in this world was like a dream. I ached for her rough touch just as much as her soft, but I had to admit that the gentleness I was experiencing surprised me. I leaned into her touch and let her caress my face.

"For someone who hung me from a ceiling only days ago, you're strangely more affectionate than I expected," I admitted. My voice was hushed.

Hale's claws pressed harder into my jawline but didn't break the skin. "I can hang you again, if you desire," she purred.

My core tingled at the thought. "Perhaps later," I replied.

"I may be a monster, but I'm not without sexual etiquette," she said. "...I cannot lie. You make me softer than I have ever wanted to be. Equally so, depravity."

Her words made me bite my bottom lip. "I want it all," I told her.

"All of you." I used my hands at the back of her neck to ease her head down more so that I could press my lips to hers. Her fangs nipped at me, and I relished in the quickly fading sting.

"You have me," Hale growled into our kiss.

I pulled back, then pecked her lips, once, then twice, then a third time. "I'm yours," I insisted. "Taken, claimed, kept... always." I leaned in to kiss her again, but noticed Hale's body stiffen.

I thought perhaps it was a reaction to our naked closeness, but she did not take my mouth nor grip me tightly in response. Her gaze had moved from me and to the wall to the left of the tub. Distant.

"Hale?" I asked. My brow knit.

After a moment, Hale finally looked down at me. "We shouldn't get too excited. I will not be able to stop myself..." she said.

My body flushed hotter than the water. "You don't have to." I was ready and willing to forget anything and everything else that existed in the universe to cling to Hale in orgasm and fluff for as long as the fates allowed. Just thinking about it made my head dizzy.

"You're tired, it was a long night," Hale cooed. Her voice was so deep and raspy that it brought goosebumps on my skin. Just at that moment, my stomach growled.

"You are famished, Little One," she added. "Let me take care of you."

I sighed and nodded, resigning myself to the needs of humankind that, oh so unfortunately, hadn't been left behind in the mortal world.

Hale slid me forward, letting go of me and removing me from her lap. She stood and stepped out with ease. The large tub felt lonely without her in it. Her fur, though not a consistent spreading along her entire body, was wet and laid flat against her skin. Her ears were the only thing dry. I watched droplets of water drip between her breasts and down her defined stomach.

My thighs squeezed together, and I clamped my mouth shut. My eyes widened as I watched the water begin to steam and evaporate off her as her eyes glowed brighter. The steam filled the room, fogging my vision for a moment before it dissipated, flowing out of the open doorway. Hale was completely dry now.

"Wow," I whispered.

"After everything that impresses you?" she asked. Her eyes with their diamond pupils squinting.

I looked down at the water with a slight chuckle. "Everything about you does," I insisted, and didn't look at her.

Suddenly the tub was draining, though Hale didn't come over and unplug it. I watched the water swirl downward until I was left dripping into the empty bath.

"Stand," Hale commanded, her voice low.

I listened, without hesitance, and realized as I stood up that I was in fact tired, as she had said. I wobbled on my feet as I looked up at her.

Hale was holding something akin to a towel, it was much, much, larger, and as she wrapped me in it I realized the fabric was much softer. The thing covered me from shoulders to ankles and my arms were crossed in front of me underneath. She scooped me up into her arms.

I smiled softly, but then looked over to the corner of the room where Fern had been the last I checked. She wasn't there.

I heard a purr below and looked down over Hale's arm to see

Fern standing at Hale's feet, looking concerned.

"We're going to bed, come on," I told her. "Everything's okay."

Hale reached down, but Fern hissed softly and stepped back, so she redirected her hand to the carrier and picked that up instead. It had only a few things in it, but the most important was some food for Fern. Hale placed the bag in my lap and started out of the room.

I placed my hands on her shoulder and eased myself up a bit more so I could see that Fern was following us. She was. From a distance. Inching, then scurrying along when we got too far away. I didn't pay attention to where we were going. The hallways all looked the same, dimly lit, black and golden tapestries here and there, but overall, rather empty.

Until we turned into the room I was familiar with. The room with the pillow and blanket nest as I had thought of it before. I was wondering if Hale even had a bed...even slept in a bed. Or, I suppose what I would consider a bed.

Perhaps the pile of plush linens was what a bed was here...

Hale set me down, and I set the carrier down as well. Fern hesitated in the large doorway.

"It's alright," I insisted, but she stayed put.

I frowned. Was I wrong for bringing her with me? I couldn't imagine leaving her with anyone else. Just the thought made my heart ache.

"She will adjust, like you will," Hale told me.

I blinked and looked up at her. Surprised that she cared, though... she had let me go after I'd told her about Fern. Perhaps the two had more in common than I realized.

I nodded, my voice feeling lost inside my chest, my head feeling heavy.

Hale unwrapped the towel from me and let it fall to the floor. I was mostly dry except for my hair, that still dripped down my back.

"Let me dress you," she insisted as she grabbed a fabric similar to the one we'd left in the field. This one was a soft plum color and as she wrapped it around me, moving my arms up, tying it behind my neck and my lower back, I noticed it was shorter. It stopped near my knees instead of my ankles.

"Thank you," I whispered. Everything felt...surreal.

Hale's fingers traced the line of my neck and shoulder, and she looked at me heatedly.

"You must rest before I take you again and again. I need to find food."

I swallowed hard, and I sat down on the edge of the nest, sinking down a few inches.

"I will," I promised. But instead of laying down, I grabbed the cat carrier, reached into a side pocket and grabbed the small bag of Fern's food. It was enough for a day or two, but I'd have to get more.

I held some in my hand and held it toward the doorway.

"Come here girl," I said sweetly, "it's okay. Come, eat."

She walked over hesitantly, walking in a zigzag line and taking careful steps. I made a soft sound with my mouth to call her in more.

Finally, she was at my hand, sniffing and tilting her head to the side. She ate a little out of my hand, and I pet her head gently. "Sweet darling," I cooed, "see, everything is okay here."

I put the rest of her food on the floor beside the makeshift bed and she ate more happily.

I looked over at Hale, who was standing a couple feet back now.

"I'll need to get her more food too," I told her, my brow knit.

I watched her eyes shift down to Fern and there was a slight contorting of her face. My stomach tightened. Did Fern bother her?

I felt a flood of protection over my cat and reached over to soothe mostly myself by running a hand over her.

"You won't be getting anything," Hale told me.

I blinked. "What?" I asked.

"You can't go back to your...the human world," she said, voice rough.

I swallowed. "You could take me anywhere. Somewhere no one knows who I am. I just need to get Fern some food and...maybe a few other things so she can survive here."

I could use some things as well...but if I had to choose Fern over myself, I had already decided.

Hale exhaled, the sound with a slight rumble. "I cannot risk it," she insisted.

My jaw tightened. The daydream like cloud over my head was falling away. I was here in this world, completely separate from the one I was born into, and I had promised myself to a monster. A beautiful monster who made me feel more alive than ever... but she held my life in her hands, and now Ferns.

"Am I allowed to leave this... place?" I asked, waving my hand around. "See more of your world?"

Hale's gaze felt distant again, but this time I knew for certain it wasn't because of our closeness.

I was accurately aware of my aching muscles now as they tightened.

"No?" I mumbled, looking away from her, but didn't expect an answer, nor did I get one. I felt the tension in the room.

"It's not safe," Hale finally said after a long moment.

I looked over and up at her again. There was something else there on her face, her lips, like she wanted to say something else.

"What aren't you telling me?" I asked. "Explain to me. Tell me more about the Midaworld, about you."

Hale looked away and was quiet.

The only sound in the room was the sound of Fern crunching away, and if I didn't feel so anxious, it may have been amusing.

"Not yet," Hale rumbled, and turned around. She strode away from me to the doorway.

"You're leaving?" I asked.

"Yes, for now," Hale told me.

"Yes," I frowned, "you can leave, but not me." My words were more spiteful than intended.

Hale turned around to look at me, eyes blazing. "'Monster mine' you called me. You'd do well to remember that I am a predator, and will do as such." Then she turned around and disappeared into the hallway.

I looked after her for a long moment, until my stomach settled, and my body didn't feel so tight.

Fern was done eating now and was rubbing against my calves, looking at me curiously.

"I'm okay," I assured her.

I wasn't sure what Hale was keeping from me, and the idea of being stuck inside was a tough one to swallow; but I was there. I'd chosen Hale, a creature who had kidnapped me in the night...who lit my very soul.

If there was one thing I was certain of, it was that there was nothing Hale could do to make me regret my decision.

10

TROUBLE IN PARADISE

Renee

I slept incredibly fucking unsoundly, but it wasn't because of the bed. That I was sure of. I felt restless in Hale's absence. Which I felt pathetic about... I'd never had trouble sleeping alone before. But remembering the way she'd left and the tension that had been left behind made me ache. It made my stomach twitch in annoyance as well. She was a monster, and she could do whatever she wanted, but that didn't mean I wasn't allowed to be upset.

I shook my head as I sat on the edge of the nest. What was I really upset about?

I didn't care all that much about not being able to go back to the human realm, but not being able to leave even this...place that Hale lived in was too much. I wanted more than to be a bird in a cage.

I wanted Hale, and I wanted her world fully, completely, in every way. Kevin and Casey could have each other, and I'd have my monster. No matter how unhinged it seemed.

With one breath, then another, I decided I was going to tell her that. If I was her mate, as she said, I wanted to be her mate. I wanted all of it. Not just four concrete walls and a pile of blankets.

Though, as I looked at the scabbed over marks on the sides of my thighs and remembered how intoxicating being taken by her was...I thought perhaps I could get used to it. As long as she was there.

Which right then she wasn't. I itched and squirmed with impatience.

Where had she gone? I was so hungry.

"Well," I whispered, "if she wanted me to stay where I am, she would have locked the door." I pushed up onto my feet. Fern was curled up within the nest of blankets and pillows, looking comfortable. Knowing she wasn't completely stressed out eased my nerves.

With that knowledge, I headed for the door that was still open. I was grateful, as I wasn't so sure I could get it open completely; it was just as massive as everything around there seemed to be.

My bare feet padded down the hallway. I wasn't sure what I was looking for...something, anything, to give me more answers about Hale and about this place. I walked casually, but with interest. I didn't feel afraid that she might come back and find me wandering around. If anything, the idea of perhaps being chased by her again was a welcome one. Even if my legs were still sore.

Unlike the first time I had been in these halls, I didn't fear for my life. I wanted to explore. I ran my fingers along the walls, feeling the smooth texture fade into a grit in some spots. In others, there seemed to be words or symbols carved into the rock. A language I could not recognize.

I found another door, and I pushed at it with my shoulder. It wouldn't budge, not even a little. Perhaps I really wasn't strong enough... I gave it another go and heard a slight rattling.

"Hm." It was locked, or I was pretty sure it was. "Curious."

I continued down the corridor while making mental notes on

which ways I had turned so that I stood a chance of being able to navigate back to the room I'd come from.

This place was beautiful. Dim lights hung from high above me, casting my shadow every which way. If the halls were so beautiful, in their own eery way, I could only imagine the possibilities of the other rooms.

"Hale." A voice echoed through the corridors. It wasn't loud, almost a whisper.

I turned, uncertain if I was hearing things. I brushed my still slightly damp hair behind my ears and focused.

"Darling, I brought the..." the voice continued, and then cut off. It was a feminine voice, sort of.

"Hells!"

Suddenly, I was slammed backwards against the wall. I gasped and whined as the hard stone hit my shoulder bones and my head knocked against it. My vision was blurry for a second.

"Fuck!" I spat. I felt two hands pinning me to the wall by my shoulders.

"Who are you?" they spoke as my vision cleared. "A little treat that got away perhaps..."

Their voice had a raspy undertone, but was smooth like a dry red wine.

I panted softly. "Let go of me!" I demanded and pushed at their petite shoulders, but they were strong. Much stronger than me, despite being only a few inches taller. They looked...more human than Hale. Not feline in the slightest. Their skin was a pallid gray, with sunken black under-eye bags and piercing yellow irises. Black horns jutted out from their forehead in one large curl and the points nearly touched my head.

They tsked me. "I thought Hale was better at tying knots," they said and bared their teeth.

Fear flew up from my stomach into my throat and tightened it as I looked at their glinting fangs. Two points are on the top, two on the bottom.

Their slender, freezing cold hand slipped to my neck.

"I didn't know they were bringing snacks home…"

I squirmed and struggled to find my voice. "I'm not—I'm not a snack," I huffed. "I'm…" before I could get the words out, they were grabbing my hair and yanking my head to the side.

I yelped, wracked my fists against them, but they were like stone.

Just as I squeezed my eyes shut, I heard a roaring growl from down the hallway.

"Madriel!" Hale yelled and suddenly they were no longer against me, and I was sliding to the floor. "She is not yours to eat!"

I was shivering as I opened my eyes, and saw Hale baring her sharp teeth in their direction as they picked themselves up off the floor.

"Don't be greedy now," the creature, Madriel, apparently, hissed.

Gale rumbled out. "She is mine." And her eyes burned brighter. "My mate."

Madriel blinked and tilted their head to the side, then looked at me. "Oh. Well, dear, you could have given me at least one bloody note about her," they growled, low and irritated. "Had I known you'd gone and claimed one of the humans, I wouldn't have behaved so rashly." They brushed their hands along their pants, smooth black velvet pants.

I was still trying to catch my breath.

"I didn't think you'd be here so soon," Hale insisted. Her gaze shifted to me, concern flickering. She knelt down and brushed her claws along my chin. A silent word of apology there.

"I suppose I should have guessed this was what you needed the wolfsbane for," Madriel said, voice disinterested. "We can discuss this later." There was a slight clink as they placed a bottle on the floor, then a rush of wind.

Madriel was gone.

And my head was still spinning.

"Who?" was all I could manage.

Hale eased me up from the floor and ran her fingers along the back of my head, where a slight bump was rising. I hissed out.

She grumbled. "One of few friends. An old one," she replied, "though if they had fed from you, they may have been a dead one."

I swallowed hard and looked up at her. "You could've warned me."

Hale narrowed her eyes. "You weren't supposed to leave the room."

With a huff, I pushed myself away from both the wall and her. "You didn't tell me to stay!" I told her. "If you'd like me to be your little pet slut, the least you could do is actually tell me." My blood felt hot. Everything felt more...intense here. Need, anger, frustration, perhaps even jealousy. "Or does my desire not matter?"

I was so caught up in my mood I didn't notice Hale was carrying something in one of her hands. Something white that crinkled every now and again.

I turned my back to her, feeling equal parts irritated and elated with the tension.

A gasp slipped from my throat as Hale's hand wrapped around my throat from behind and forced me back against her as she leaned down. Her fingers forced my head to tilt back, and I stared up into her face.

"You are mine," she growled. "...but I will not force myself upon you. Do not fool yourself with this...anger at my protection of you."

I shivered. "Is it really protection?" I asked. I bristled at the silence that followed, and then Hale turned me around completely and lifted me into the air with one swoop of her arm around my waist.

"Little One, why do your emotions taste so delicate?" she asked with a rumble, "...you are on fire with me."

It took a moment for me to realize she was asking why I was upset with her.

My face reddened, and I squirmed like a small animal caught in a cage.

"You came back to me yourself," Hale reminded me.

I curled my fingers against her chest as my eyes burned. I wanted to yell at her and be held by her at the same time.

There was a bit of a thud to the floor, and I realized she had dropped something. I looked down and saw half of a bag of cat food peaking out of a crumpled white paper bag.

"You left to get things for Fern?" I asked, my voice thick. And I found myself slamming my fist down onto her shoulder. "You could have just told me!"

Now I was wriggling against her hold while cursing under my breath.

I was set to my feet, and I stumbled back a step.

"I told you I was leaving," Hale said, her eyes narrow.

I groaned and tossed my arms into the air. "You're making me so..." I curled my hands into fists. At the same moment, my thighs burned hot. Anger and arousal mixed so intoxicatingly and my head was swimming.

"I don't know how to feel!" I panted. "Even knowing you're different, knowing I have to get used to this new...life... I want to...I...I want to yell I want..." I put my hands in my hair and looked at the floor.

Hale moved closer. "You want to fight with me."

"No! I..." I looked up, expecting to see anger, but saw her...grinning, wildly, eyes burning.

"You're hot with emotion, my small fiery," Hale growled. She knelt so our faces were aligned. "You ache for the sensations you felt when we first met. Spitting angry. Tied and restrained through your lashing out."

A shiver ran up my spine.

"Here, you do not have to hide it." Hale dragged a claw along my jawline, sharp enough to end me if she wanted. "You cannot scare me. Gnash and yell at me as you like, I will not run."

My breath pushed out of me. "Hale," I all but whimpered. "...I'm...I'm good, I can be good." Tears threatened to leak onto my cheeks. "I don't want to fight, I'm a good person."

She hissed under her breath and finally gripped me wholly and pulled me to her, face inches from mine.

"But you do not have to be," she whispered. Voice raspy and low. "Everything they told you was wrong with you. That he didn't like, I will devour. Your want to fight with me, to stir my upset and be punished...here it is not wrong. Here you are free from mortal judgment. Here you do not need to feel guilt. Here I beg you, tell me everything you think and feel, in love and in anger, even that shames you. Hold you gently or chase you as prey, I will do both and delight in what you share with me, because you are my mate."

My hands were shaky, and tears dripped down my chin and soaked into my dress.

Ironically enough, the anger and frustration I had been feeling was fading. I felt overwhelmed by the affection and complete devotion. Hale, a literal monster, was showing me. Something no man or woman on earth had ever come close to.

"Hale," I whispered, and this time finally spoke without feeling like I was choking. "This is all so fucking much." I laughed behind my veil of tears and tossed my arms around her neck. Her night black hair lying gently over my arms.

"I wanted to fight with you. Like, really...argue because I was genuinely upset with you, but also because...it's the hottest thing I've ever felt. Yes. Both of those things."

I took a deep breath.

"I want to take you as you are, too. With no judgment. But I'm..." I swallowed and shook my head.

Hale looked into my blurry eyes and tilted her head to the side.

"You are not a monster," she crooned. "You are human. You are upset by things I am not. That will not change..." Her gaze shifted away, thoughtful, as her arms tightened around me. "No, I will not ask it to," she said, as though she'd been considering within her own thoughts.

Her fingers brushed my tears away. "I have never cared when I saw tears," Hale mumbled. "But seeing them on your face, I find myself considering their cause."

My brow furrowed, and I was uncertain of how it pertained to the subject, but I did not speak.

"There are certain things, certain...human things, I must adjust to with you," she said.

I looked at the floor. "Like, tell me you were going to get what I needed instead of letting me go, for my protection?" I asked.

She hummed. "Yes. But understand, Little One, I will always be a creature from the Midaworld, following my nature," Hale said, voice quiet. Our eyes were locked on each other.

My tongue darted along my lips. "I know," I whispered. I knew no other way to express how I felt besides leaning in and pressing my lips to hers. The kiss was soft, but quickly deepened and I was drawn into her and her powerful arms and body.

My fingers tangled in the hair at the nape, and she moaned into my mouth.

The kiss drew on for what felt like an eternity. Time was not and did not feel the same here. It was as though minutes passed with no effort.

Finally, Hale drew back, panting softly, teeth bared for a moment.

"Little One," she purred, "...before we get caught up... there is something we must talk about."

I pulled my floating head back down to...Midaworld as much as possible. "We've discussed quite a bit already," I chuckled.

Hale did not reply. Instead, she let go of me and grabbed the bag off the floor. Plus, whatever Madriel had brought.

"Come, follow."

I did as she asked and realized she was taking me back to the room with the nest for a bed. Fern would likely still be there, so that made sense. "Will I have somewhere else to sleep, eventually?" I asked, my fingers curling into her forearm as we walked. She was taking slower, smaller steps.

"Yes. If that is what you desire. It will take time, we can do more about it later," she said. I got the impression whatever it was we needed to talk about was more important than potential furnishings and things to make me more comfortable.

I walked over and sat down on the edge of the nest. Fern was standing, her ears alert and gaze trained on Hale. "It's alright. She got you some more food." I reached out and stroked Fern's back. Once, then twice, and she finally relaxed. She walked around in a circle thrice before laying back down again. Hale set the bag down on the floor before crawling into the center of the nest.

"What is that?" I asked, motioning to the vial of a hazy gray liquid in her hand.

Hale tilted it and it shimmered slightly, changing for a split second or two into green and violet, then it was gray once more.

"It is for a ritual," Hale said, and her eyes locked to mine. Her face was knit in extreme seriousness. It made my eyebrows pull together, and I scooted beyond the edge and closer to her in the center of the pile of pillows and blankets.

"Tell me," I insisted.

Hale's forked tongue clicked once. "I need to claim you," she said.

I blinked, and my face was warm. "Trust me, you have me." I chuckled.

She shook her head. "No. What I speak of is more than our sexual and emotional bond, as strong as it is," she says low, "...there is a ritual in which I can claim you. Bind our very essence together so tightly it cannot be undone and screams to the others that you are not theirs to touch."

My pulse quickened, and along with this was a distinct tightness at my core that only grew the more my curiosity did.

"What does this ritual consist of, exactly?" I asked.

"It can be a dangerous thing," Hale told me, "No one claiming is the same, but physical and spiritual nature of it is exhausting to all participants, and others look upon them."

I rolled over her words in my head. "Others watch the ritual?"

Hale nodded, her eyes swirling with darkness and heat as she eyed me for my reaction.

"How is it dangerous? I could...die?" A lump formed in my throat.

"Death is unlikely," Hale assured me, "...however, there have been a few humans in the past who could not handle it. They did not die, but they were not the same."

I swallowed hard and looked to the side.

"You need to know...it has been many years since claiming a human as a mate was common place here. It is not disallowed, but there are some who would rather see me end you, or wish to end you themselves. Humans are seen as a danger, as you know. In this way, claiming you is even more important," Hale explained.

I reached for her hand. "Doing this would...make it more safe for me here?" I finally looked back at her.

"This realm is dark and possessive, as am I as one of its residents.

If you desire to know more of me, of the Midaworld outside these walls, we must claim each other at the Harvest." Hale's fingers slide into the side of my hair and held me, but did not pull.

My heart and the arousal between my thighs fluttered. Hale had already done more for me than anyone I had ever cared for in the past had done. I would have to truly say goodbye to earth at some point, put it behind me...and I found I was willing to step closer to this for Hale.

I was certain of my decision as I pulled closer to her and pressed my lips to her black ones. I whispered. "Claim me."

11

MADRIEL FASHION EXTRAORDINAIRE

Renee

"What exactly is the *'Harvest'*?" I asked as Hale's fingers gently trailed along my neck. We had been lying there together for what felt like hours. I was starving, stomach growling, but I didn't want to move or even dare ask for something to eat. I didn't want her to leave my side again. So, I did my best to hide any of my needs that couldn't be sated with her touch.

Hale's hand trailed from my neck to my shoulder and down to my waist. The press of her claws and pads of her fingers brought a flush under the fabric of each spot they caressed.

"Harvest is a gathering that happens twice per year before the most succulent feeding nights of the year," Hale explained, "...the realms and their energies align in such a way that whether blood, soul, or emotion is fed on, it is most decadent."

I didn't need to imagine what Hale looked like hunting and stalking her prey, I already knew. Blazing eyes and bared teeth. Hot grasping hands and aching flesh. Except I imagined most of the humans were left in much worse shape than I. My brow furrowed for a moment, but I shoved the concern down.

"It's a very important event then," I mused. "Does the claiming ritual have to happen on that night?"

I brushed several tresses of her hair behind her pointed ear that twitched at my touch. Admiring the deep red of her skin that was darker as it grew closer to each scattered patch of raven colored fur. I noticed in that moment the thick, studded piercings in her ears. Four of them, one in her lobe and three placed seemingly haphazardly along the cartilage. The metal was black, but when the light caught it, it gave off a green shift.

"It happens traditionally during the Harvest," Hale replied, but her voice trailed off into a low hum.

I was distracted now as I ran my fingers along her ear, following the curves and circling the piercings.

"If you continue to touch me like this, you will continue to starve for a while longer. I may have to tie you up," Hale crooned.

I slid my fingers down from her ear to her neck and brushed my nails along her skin. No where near as sharp as her own, but based on her purring, low and vibrating against me, she liked it.

"I'm okay," I insisted. "I can wait to eat, but perhaps you could...indulge, while tying me up."

In a flash, I was on my back, and Hale pressed down against me. Her lips found mine and our teeth clashed together as I kissed her back, feeling the stinging pin pricks of her teeth nicking my tender flesh.

Her body was heavy on mine, pinning me down and holding me there. I wrapped my arms over her shoulders and parted my thighs wide for her to rest between. Her mouth tasted of iron and something distinctly her. Each time we kissed, my entire mouth, lips, and tongue burned softly, as if her saliva contained capsaicin.

"Hale," I moaned into her mouth.

When she finally pulled away from me, she had left my lips gently swollen and reddened. I stared into her eyes, seeing her blown out pupils mirroring mine.

Just as I leaned up to kiss her again, my stomach growled angrily. I sighed.

"I must feed you," Hale told me. "As much as I would rather string you up and feast upon you."

I squeezed my thighs against her, as if to keep her between them, but I was no match for her strength.

"If you insist," I whispered. "What can I eat here?" I tilted my head and watched hale as she parted from me and climbed out of the nest. I rolled onto my side before sitting up.

Hale narrowed her eyes. "I must leave again to obtain some food for you, not to the mortal realm," she explained, "...I do not partake in physical food very often, so there is little here."

I chewed on the inside of my cheek as I felt the hunger pains crackling and tingling up from my stomach into my throat. "Will it be as strange as what you fed me before?"

Hale looked away from me, her eyes distant with thought. "Meat will be the most familiar," she decided, "*cardak*... bread, as well."

She turned from me and then looked over her shoulder. "I will be asking Madriel for their help in preparing you for the Harvest," she told me, "...they may arrive before I return. Do not be alarmed."

Fern climbed into my lap as I sat at the edge of the nest. I pet her, partially for my own comfort, and focused on the softness and warmth of her fur.

"As long as they don't slam me against a wall again," I replied quietly. "I prefer you were the only one to do that." I lifted a hand to touch the slight bump at the back of my head, it throbbed and I winced.

Hale growled under her breath. "Yes, as would I. They will not touch you again. Trust me."

I nodded. "Thank you for telling me." Rather than leaving me not knowing what was going on, again.

Hale nodded back at me and then disappeared out of the room, leaving me with just Fern once more.

"This is strange, isn't it?" I said, looking down at her. She was kneading my thigh.

I smiled softly. "At least you're doing better." I wasn't sure what I'd do if Fern couldn't handle it here in this new place. She was used to moving from apartment to apartment with me the last five years, but this was completely different.

I sucked in a shaky breath and continued to lavish her in affections and gently praises until she decided she wanted to go back into the middle of the bed.

"You really like this nest, huh?" I asked. I couldn't help but chuckle. I understood more now about Hale and why the bed was the way it was.

I sat watching Fern for a few minutes, at least I think it's only a few minutes. There's no clock anywhere and I'm not sure if "minutes" was the right thing to use. Regardless, as I'm about to lay back down, I heard a familiar voice across the room.

"I'm here to slut you up."

I blinked and looked at the doorway with surprise. Madriel was standing there, leaning against the frame with their arms folded. Looking much less angry and terrifying than before.

"Excuse me?" I asked while standing up and brushing the skirt of my dress down. As they motioned me closer with a crooked finger, I was suddenly aware of the fact that I was not wearing a single thing under the thin plum fabric. Still, I stepped closer, hesitantly.

"I'm here to be your tailor for the Harvest," Madriel explained, "you'll need something much less...or perhaps much more, inviting to wear. Hale is not anyone would call "fashion forward" in any manner, alas, I am here."

They unfold their arms and mime down their body with a slender hand, their nails long and blood red. My eyes had a mind of their own as they trailed down them and took in their attire. Shiny black corset that clung to a flat chest and was pinned to a flowing black skirt with slits at the sides. Various bangles and bands of fabric and metal lined their arms and fingers, as well as their neck, where spikes shot out from the choker to an almost deadly length. Their feet were adorned with platforms that had teeth, perhaps actual teeth, lining the outer edges.

"Uh," I mumbled and looked back up into their face. My shoulders were tense as I thought about how they'd pinned me and nearly taken a chunk of my neck out.

"Alright. Hale says I can trust you."

Madriel chuckled, a colder sound than Hale's. "But can I trust you?" they ask. "After all, my dear friend kept you a secret until now." They cocked their head.

"It was all...sudden," I told them.

"As I hear," Madriel waves a hand. "Frankly, I'm questioning their judgment, but I'm here regardless, pet."

I glare at them. "It's Renee."

"Well, Renee, follow me. I need a room with more light." Madriel motions me.

I look back at Fern, who is sleeping, before following them out of the room and down the hallway the opposite direction I had explored in. I watched their back nervously as we walked, uncertain what to think about them. I wanted to ask them about how they knew Hale, but...I wasn't sure where to start. I had so very little idea of how the Midaworld worked beyond the dark and hungry natures that Hale told me about.

What was life like for those who lived here? Did schools and places to visit exist in the same capacity?

Madriel pushed open one side of a double door with ease and waited for me to head in before them. I was pulled from my thoughts as I entered and looked around. It was a much larger room with a wide expanse of mostly empty bookshelves. Along the top of the room were large red tinted windows, or perhaps the light peering through was red. It lit up the room much brighter than I had ever seen and allowed me to see just how devilish Madriel was as I turned to face them. They looked even more sullen and exhausted in color, but a slight sparkle glinted off their long, flowing purple hair that was pulled up in elaborate twists and braids.

"Now, climb up and stand still," they ordered as they pulled over a dusty ottoman. They clicked their tongue. "Hale could really stand to redecorate and actually use this place to its potential," they murmured.

I stepped up and sunk down slightly on the cushion. My eyes darted around to take in more of the room. From what I had seen, there wasn't a lot going on in the massive stone house Hale and now

I called home. It seemed Hale didn't use a majority of the rooms or furnishings, nor have much company. It made me wonder just how she spent her time.

"I said stand still," Madriel repeated. "That includes your head, darling."

My ears flushed, and I put my chin straight ahead, arms at my sides. My eyes darted around to watch them move. They pulled what appeared to be a tape measure of some sort out of thin air.

"How long have you known Hale?" I asked as they took in my height first.

Madriel mumbled something in a language I did not recognize and then motioned for me to lift my arms. I did as instructed and tensed as I felt the tape touch my back and spread along my shoulders.

"A long time," they replied simply. "Longer than a human such as you could understand."

My face twisted gently. "I'm here willingly, so... I understand more than you give me credit for."

They sighed from behind me and continued their work. Despite the rather intimate feeling of having my measurements taken, they didn't actually touch me even once. Their fingers were quick and nimble as they moved and didn't brush me or assist me in moving. Only the tape measure touched me for the briefest moments.

"You cannot truly understand the risk being here poses," Madriel replied as they moved in front of me. "I assure you, it's beyond even your darkest fantasies." Their eyes narrowed and there was a flicker of emotion in them. I may have even thought it was pain if I wasn't heated with annoyance at their dismissal.

I huffed softly. "If you're so against my being here, why are you doing this?" I asked.

Madriel stopped for a moment and tilted their head to the side. At this same moment, I saw Hale appear in the doorway and my tense shoulders relaxed some.

"Because they know I would do the same," Hale answered my question. She was holding what appeared to be a bowl in one of her hands as she walked over to us.

"Hale," I whispered in relief. I started to step down from the ottoman, but Madriel stepped closer and hissed quietly.

"Stay," they said.

I glared and curled my toes into the cushion underneath them.

"I know you would do the same, in a manner of speaking," Madriel told Hale, looking to the side, "...though we both know you would not be in charge of the fashion if the roles were reversed."

Hale stepped closer to me, her eyes full of affection and curiosity. "Are you alright?" she asked.

I frowned. "I'm hungry, and your friend is pushy." I shook my head. "I know, things are different here, I should expect it."

I notice now that what she's holding is a bowl that steams slightly. The scent of something...spiced and rich overwhelms my senses and my mouth waters.

"What is that?" I asked, leaning toward it ever so slightly.

"Food," Hale told me, "...it is the quickest thing I could find on short notice that wouldn't require a night of tending to."

I raised an eyebrow, but looking into the bowl of thick red, orange and purple ingredients only made my stomach growl.

Hale lifted a wooden spoon full, and it dripped slightly. "Taste, eat." She lifted it to my face and took the spoon in my mouth with no hesitation.

A strange, hot sensation of flavors exploded over my tongue and tingled down my throat. A taste similar to poultry was there, as well as an earthy starchy taste root vegetables. I chewed and swallowed and relished in the hot food going down my throat. I opened my mouth again and was greeted with another bite. On this second bite, I noticed a slightly bittersweet undertone, similar to the dessert I'd had. On the third bite, the heat really kicked in and my eyes watered, but I couldn't get enough of it.

"Not to interrupt this lovely little scene, but I need to finish..." Madriel said.

I'd almost forgotten they were there. I licked my lips and whined slightly as Hale pulled the spoon away and took a step back.

"Fine, but this outfit for the harvest better be worth it," I told them.

Madriel scoffed. "Don't you dare doubt me. We've only just met, but surely you can see I'm the better dressed of all three of us."

I moved my lips down and eyebrows up in an expression that said "you're not wrong."

Madriel continued to measure me, a bit more closely to my thighs and hips. I caught Hale's gaze, and it was jealous and hungry. My face caught fire, and I did my best not to squirm.

"Done," Madriel said and turned to Hale. "Though I don't think this is a good idea." They tacked on.

I stayed where I stood, watching Hale and them interact. Despite Hale being several feet taller than Madriel, Madriel moved with seemingly effortless grace and confidence. Even while looking up at

Hale, they did not appear submissive or unequal to them in strength or power. The only sign of any weakness was how tired and pained their eyes were whenever they looked at me.

"Claiming her is the best way to keep her safe," Hale insisted.

Madriel snapped their fingers, and the tape measure disappeared to where it had come. My head spun with the implications and possibilities. What was Madriel? What other beings and abilities existed?

"The best way, perhaps, but not a done deal," they said, and their voice became more hushed. Just loud enough that I could hear. "You know how this ended for me."

I watched Hale's body stiffen and her eyes simply locked with Madriel's, exchanging something silent for a moment.

"I know," she said slowly, "and I require your trust. I would never think..."

Madriel cut her off. "Think that you are more capable than keeping your own pet safe than I?" they huffed softly and turned halfway toward the door. They lifted a hand. "I won't stop you from this, and against my better judgment, I'll have the dress to you in time for Harvest."

Nothing else was said as Madriel left the room.

"Can I sit now?" I asked.

Hale looked over at me. "Yes, Little One."

As I moved to sit on the ottoman instead of standing, Hale crouched down at eye level with me. I reached for the bowl, but she moved it back an inch. "It's hot," she insisted. Though she held it in her hand with ease. Instead, she gave me the spoon and held the bowl for me.

There was something domestic about it as I eagerly continued to eat from the bowl she held for me. Keeping it steady and still and not wavering even once as I ate. She simply watched me with a curious eye.

I was thoroughly distracted by filling my stomach, and the once overwhelming heat became a familiar taste that eased into something that more so tingled at the edges of my lips and throat rather than scalded them.

"This is really good," I said, almost done with the rather large bowl. My stomach was sloshing and aching from how full it was. It was delightful. "Dare I ask what it is?"

"You wouldn't know what I said if I told you," Hale said, "...if you knew what the creature you are eating looked like, you might be less inclined." There was a wicked look in her eyes.

I licked at my lips and looked back into the bowl. It looked like food to me. Perhaps the color variants were different and the texture of the meet didn't align with the taste in a completely cohesive manner that I was used to, but I was fond of it at that moment.

"I will trust you on that," I replied and continued eating.

As I put the last spoonful in my mouth, Hale took it from me and set the bowl to the side.

"Are you satisfied, my mate?" she asked.

I smiled. My belly was full and head sleepy. I scooted over to her, halfway off the ottoman, and wrapped my arms around one of hers. "Yes, very."

She hummed and brushed several curls behind my ear. The tips of her claws against my ear made me shiver and close my eyes. I want to kiss her, to be taken and take as we did in the clearing the night...or nights before, I wasn't sure... but I was too full. So I sat in silence for a long moment until I was finally carried away to rest.

12

THE ONE WITH THE LIBRARY

Renee

My body squirmed against the ropes that secured me to the ceiling. They were wrapped and knotted around my thighs and hips, snaking their way up my torso and parting my breasts. The way I dangled caused the perfect amount of pressure on my aching flesh. I tilted my head back and let it just hang there, my hair draping down.

"Good Little One," Hale purred. She stood behind me and brushed her claws along my cheek. "Waiting so patiently." She spun me so that my thighs, which were tied open, spreading me for her, was facing her. I had been waiting for this moment for what I was certain was days.

Sleep there was strange, I wasn't sure how much time had passed, nor if it was truly day or night; but after getting as much rest as I could and more food, Hale was finally convinced I was prepared for what she wanted to do with me. What I ached for.

Hale came closer, but I couldn't see her, only sense her. I felt her hot breath on my skin and soon her forked tongue trailed from my knee to the inside of my thigh. I shivered and wriggled against my bindings.

She did not have to crouch or lean to reach my wet pussy, no, because I was suspended at the level of her head, far above the floor.

Perhaps in the past it would've frightened me, but right then I only felt pure elation. My skin prickled with goosebumps and my thighs tensed as I awaited more from her.

"My Little Prey," Hale praised me, her voice a husky growl, "my pretty little prey, that's what you want to be, isn't it?" Her hands slid onto my thighs, pushing them slightly farther apart, and I strained against the ropes.

"Yes," I replied, already breathless.

"Say it." Hale flicked her tongue at the apex of my thigh and groin, and my hips twitched.

I tilted my head up so I could look at her for just a moment. See her bright red eyes so captivating and full of desire. "I'm your pretty little prey," I whined.

"Good Girl." Hale wasted no time diving in, her tongue penetrated my pussy with ease, sliding in inch by inch until I was full.

I gasped, feeling myself already pulsing and clenching around her. I struggled to rock my hips against her face, unable to move much at all. Her claws grazed my labia and the pads of her fingers settled on my clit, caressing the sensitive nub in slow circles.

"Hale," I moaned, my body squirming needily.

With each passing moment, the bubble of pleasure and need built up in my stomach. As she ate me out, her tongue finding my most sensitive spots, I cried and moaned into the echo chamber of a room.

Her tongue slipped free for just a moment. "That's it, Little One," she growled, "let me taste you drip, your pretty little cunt is so delectable."

"Oh, God!" My entire body tensed, toes curling, as she thrust her tongue in and out of me again and again. Her fingers massaged my clit in such wild but expert motions. Every single thought left my head, not a one remained for me to hang onto as I was driven over the edge.

My pussy clenched, again and again, and I gushed onto her face and hands. Hale only indulged in me harder and faster, not relenting even as I shook and cried as I orgasmed.

"Hale oh...Mistress, oh...my...fuck!" I panted for air as though I had been drowning.

I felt her fingers pressed against my entrance and stiffened; I expected more pain, given her claws, but as her large strong fingers slid into my cunt, I only felt a stinging pressure. I realized suddenly that the hand she had slipped inside me was covered with something, a glove perhaps. Keeping her sharp claws from truly hurting me. I could still feel the overwhelming heat of her as she plunged her fingers in and out and her tongue lashed at my clit.

"I need...I," I tried to talk, so dizzy, mouth so...dry. I wasn't even sure what I was going to say.

"Hold on, just one more Little One. Cum for me one more time." She continued to fuck me with her fingers and bring me closer with her tongue. The air in the room was stifling and moist as I struggled to breathe it in.

"B-Bite me," I begged. "Bite..." I didn't have to finish my request.

Suddenly I was hit with burning and searing pain on the inside of my thigh. Hale's teeth sunk into my flesh with ease. The pain sent a shiver up my body and my eyes rolled back. I could hear her growling against my skin.

Her teeth left me, and I felt warmth dripping from my thigh.

"Hale!" I cried. Every ounce of pleasure I had to feel and give clenched inside of my stomach and quivered down my thighs. My pussy throbbed along with my clit as I went rigid and breathless. My body ached to ride my orgasm out harder, faster, and Hale made up for my lack of movement by thrusting her fingers in harder.

Finally, I couldn't take anymore. My body relaxed, slumped really, as my juices dripped from my swollen folds to the floor. I felt the full weight of my body against the ropes now, much heavier than before. They dug in uncomfortably, but the bliss swirling around in my head made it easy not to care.

I flinched as Hale slid one of her un-gloved knuckles along my pussy, collecting some of my wet arousal.

"Taste," Hale insisted, and shoved her knuckle and a good majority of her curled finger into my mouth. "Taste what I taste. How delicious you are! My perfect mate."

I sucked at her finger, tasting the musky desire of me, and it caused my hips to buck up in a small, limited motion.

"Mmm," I hummed out.

Everything was an empty dizzy hazy blur for a few moments there. My body was the heaviest paperweight to exist. Until I felt the ropes being cut and torn from my body.

"No patience for untying," Hale crooned, and suddenly I was in her arms, nestled against her chest. She was clothed still. I brushed my fingers against her.

"Let me...help, you," I said. My voice was small and quiet.

"This was about you, pet," she said. "Do not touch me."

I did as she asked and did not attempt to please her as she pleased me. I simply allowed her to carry me to the bathroom and bathe me as she had days before. I was already becoming accustomed to this tradition. The hot water, the inviting, clean scent, and her hands washing me with more compassion and care than a single human being ever had.

"What is the smell?" I asked as I was being dried off and sitting on the edge of the tub. "The one you put in the water." I felt more clear minded now and less like I was floating in space.

Hale slid my dress on my body and I moved my arms and head when needed.

"It is an oil that comes from...*suguisador*," she said, and I was uncertain. She met my confused eyes.

"...the blood tree," Hale explained. Though I was only left with more curiosities.

"Why is it called that?" I asked. "I want to know more about this place."

Hale hummed. "It grows in places of heavy bloodshed. I might have some books," she said. I suddenly remembered the sparse library with space for hundreds of books.

"It didn't look like you have many," I frowned. "I'd love for some fiction as well. I know I can't go back; but I wish I'd been able to bring books with me." Or that I had actually dived in and bought that eReader. Though, would I even be able to charge it there?

I brushed that thought away as I noticed Hale was picking me up again.

"I can walk to the library, you know," I chuckled. "You don't have to carry me everywhere."

Hale gave me a dark look. "I will carry you if I desire." She paused as we got to the doorway. "And you are right. As far as your world knows, you are missing or dead, but it is still not safe for you to return."

I sighed and leaned my head against my shoulder. "Do you think we will need to...provide some sort of ending for me? To the world?" I mused. "Or will I just be missing forever?"

Hale didn't answer me right away, instead carrying me down the corridor in silence.

"Who is there who will miss you?" she responded finally.

My face contorted sightly. "Few I guess." It was a harsh reality. "As least it didn't feel like it. I'll miss a few people. My coworker Maryanne. She's a nice girl." I smiled weakly. "I might even miss fighting with my dad a little."

Hale stopped and looked down at me. My eyes were wet. Her mouth shifted from a straight line to almost a frown.

"But I want this," I assured her and caressed along her collarbones. "I...feel like I would choose you, even if I had an entire world of people who cared about me." I looked down, feeling guilty. Shame. Would I really run to Hale, run to the darkness of the Midaworld if I had a loving and active family who made me feel safe and cared about?

There was no way to know; but I couldn't imagine not being drawn to Hale.

"No shame," Hale whispered. "You are strong and the fire that ignites my every sense. We are meant to be together."

I look up into her face as she continued walking. "You really believe that?"

She looked up from me and kept her eyes in front of us. "You are my mate. I would find you in any universe."

My face flushed deeply, and I nuzzled against her tighter, feeling her arms shift underneath me. Just as I realize that we've been walking an oddly long time for going to the library, there's a flicker of darkness and glimmer all around us, and suddenly we are somewhere else.

"What the..." I gasped softly, startled. When I looked around, I saw different but familiar stone walls. They were a slightly lighter gray, and the floor underneath Hale's feet was covered in a long ornate shimmering black rug that went on forever and ever — or was layered masterfully.

"Where are we?" I asked, looking over Hale's shoulder the best as I could.

"Madriel has a much bigger collection than me," Hale explained. It took me a second to realize she was talking about books.

I heard a door close to the left of us. "You could give a bitch more notice, you know," Madriel's voice came from far, and then they were over to us in a flash. They were wrapped in a silky navy blue robe with fluffy sleeves and hem.

"Renee wants books to read," Hale explained, partially.

Madriel tsked. "And your poor excuse for a library couldn't satisfy her if it tried," they sighed, "very well. But I'll not have you getting frisky in there."

Hale set me down with little warning. My bare feet touched the rug, and it was much softer than the floor at Hale's.

"You would do better to show her around," Hale said. It wasn't a question, and Madriel didn't seem to like that.

"Show her around Madriel, oh please Madriel, thank you

Madriel," they mocked and gave Hale an icy glare.

I place my hand on Hale's arm. "I'd like if you showed me around, Madriel," I said with a strained smile. I still wasn't sure what I thought about them. They clearly didn't think I was a good choice.

Madriel hummed. "Alright. But next time, give me more than a thought's notice."

They motioned me forward, and I looked at Hale. "Go," she said. "I must make more food for you whilst you look."

My brow furrowed, but I nodded and turned away from her to follow Madriel. When I looked behind my shoulder again a few steps later, she was gone.

She trusted Madriel, or she wouldn't leave me alone with them, but I still felt nervous.

My eyes darted to Madriel's back for a moment, noticing the sway of their hips in a passing glance before I looked in front of me again. I was more and more curious about how the two of them knew each other. Madriel had made it clear they had known each other for a very long time.

I wasn't so sure I should ask about it again.

Madriel pushed open the double doors into a room filled with golden orange and red light that poured down from hanging crystal lanterns. Each wall was at least ten feet tall with deep brown book-shelves filled to the almost entirely to the brim. Only a few spots for new content seemed to remain. The lounge chairs and couches in the middle of the room didn't interest me much, as my focus was on the sparkling golden and silver spines.

My mouth may as well have been hanging open. "Wow."

"Do tell dear, what are you looking for?" Madriel asked. I looked over to see them lay themselves over a chair and crossed their long, slender legs.

I pulled myself together. "Uh, well...I'd like to know more about the Midaworld."

Madriel rolled their eyes. "That narrows it down to only about one hundred books," they replied, "many of which are not in a language you will understand."

I frowned. "I just...want to know what it's like here. What other creatures live here, why does this placed exist?" I stepped closer to them.

They pursed their lips. "Well. I suppose if you can get Hale to read to you...it would be best to start with..." Madriel was suddenly out of the chair and on the other side of the room, standing on a bookshelf ladder and running their fingers along some books. "Ah." They pulled one out and rushed over to me.

I jumped slightly. "Fuck."

Madriel smirked. "Get used to it." They held the book out to me. It was only an inch thick and fit comfortably in both of my hands. The cover was pitch dark and several words were scrawled across the front in blood red ink that glistened when I tilted the book. The spine was woven with a similar color.

"Thank you," I smiled softly. I set the book down on a cushion nearby. Madriel's eyes flitted over to it.

"Do be careful with the books I am so graciously lending you. I've been collecting longer than you can imagine," they told me.

My face flushed. "From both realms?" I asked. They looked at me with a chuckle.

"Of course. Is there something else you're looking for?" They tilted their head to the side.

I lick my lips. "Well, fiction would be nice. I didn't exactly get to bring my collection here. It's...much smaller, of course."

"No doubt," Madriel leans against a chair. "Be more specific."

I spoke confidently. "Romance."

They nodded and looked thoughtful as they stood up straight. "There is plenty here to be sure," they confirmed, "though I'm surprised Hale is even leaving you with time to read romance."

Although my ears were hot, I tried not to show that I was flustered. I looked around. "Where then?" I asked.

"That depends, are you looking for tender and innocent, or something to titillate?" they asked.

I followed their graceful steps as they moved along the shelves. Everything was so beautiful. The room absolutely breathed life and knowledge, I couldn't decide where to look and when to rip my eyes from one shelf to the next.

The room smelled of vintage tomes and roses.

"Both," I replied, "but let's go with the second for now."

Madriel stopped and slid the ladder over to me. "Second shelf. Mind your step, I don't need blood on the floor."

I chuckled weakly and headed up the ladder carefully. It was difficult with my bare feet, but the ladder was wooden and the steps were wider than normal. I brushed my fingertips along the books, reading the names of the ones in English. I recognized many of them and smiled.

"Wow, some of these look like...first additions," I mused.

"They are," Madriel said from below.

I giggled, my head spinning with the possibilities of having so many books at my disposal. So long as Madriel didn't change their mind.

"Oh, no way!" I pulled a book out. "They stopped printing this one after only two weeks in 1953. I tried for months to find a copy online a few years ago, but never could." I turned the sapphic vampire romance over in my hands. It looked like it had been hardly touched, and it almost felt wrong to open it up and look at the ink of the text.

I would have been dancing if I wasn't on the ladder, so I simply wiggled my hips in delight and placed the book on the lip of the shelf before looking at the others.

With excitement bursting at my edges, I grabbed a few more before looking down to see if Madriel was still there. They were a few feet away, looking at their nails. I realized suddenly that they could see up my dress, but...they didn't seem to be looking, or complaining.

They're monsters, for fuck's sake, I think the last thing they care about is seeing your bare ass. I reminded myself. I climbed down the ladder, carefully holding a few books in one of my arms.

"Fuck yes, I can't wait to read these," I beamed. "Maybe it won't be so hard to adjust here after all." I bounced on my toes slightly before taking the books over to where the other, perhaps more important one, was sitting.

"I don't want to take too many," I said. "I'm...really grateful that you're letting me take any at all." I told Madriel. I felt their eyes on me as I looked around the room, daring myself to look at nothing else.

They stepped closer, I could feel their presence, colder than Hale's.

"You know, I'm seeing why Hale is so drawn to you," they said.

I blinked and looked over at them. "What?"

"Why they're so obsessed with you. Believing you to be their mate," Madriel "I can see why." Their gaze shifts down and then up and they squint.

My face flushes. "If I didn't know any better, I'd say you were interested," I told them, my throat tight, "...you tried to bite me before. I don't think Hale would like what you're saying." I took a half step back.

Madriel suddenly laughed and stepped closer to me, placing a hand on my waist, and a chill ran up my spine.

"Oh dove, I didn't want to fuck you, I wanted to eat you." They flashed their fangs. "I'm not interested in the pleasures you partake in with Hale." They removed their hand.

My ears grew hotter. "I see," I replied. "That's...good." My voice was uncertain.

"I mean...not that you want to eat me. I'm not interested in being...dinner either," I replied. "I don't imagine that would end well."

Madriel clicked their tongue. "We will never know, will we?" Their eyes shifted to the side. "Hale, back so soon?"

13

EMOTIONS

Hale

My eyes landed on Renee and then Madriel second. I stood at the doorway just long enough to see their hand on my mate. Briefly, I wondered what they had been talking about, seeing a look of relief on Renee's face when she realized I was there. If I didn't know Madriel was disinterested in sex, I might have thought the touch was less than innocent.

I knew they would not feed from Renee, not unless she asked them too, and based on the way she hurriedly gathered books into her arms and came over to me, I doubted her interest in that greatly.

"She needs to eat," I replied simply. Madriel didn't ask or poke and prod for any other information. I turned my attention to Renee, who stood beside me. "Did you find what you wanted?"

She smiled, and I swore her eyes glittered. "Yes! Oh, there's so many amazing books, I'm going to fucking devour these." She hopped slightly.

I could feel her excitement and happiness flutter from her body in a warm, engulfing wave. It sunk into me, asking me to taste it, and I did, with a gentle shiver. I looked at her hungrily. "As will I, with you," I said.

Renee flushed deeply and held the books tighter.

I tore my eyes away from her and looked at Madriel, who was smirking.

"Thank you for allowing her access to your library," I said with a nod of my head.

Madriel waves a hand nonchalantly. "It's no trouble. But if I don't get those back in perfect condition, you will pay dearly." They squinted.

"As always," I replied. "Next time, I will give more notice."

They gave me a look of appreciation. "Get going now. I'll have the dress done soon enough."

With that, I swept Renee off her feet once more and into my arms. She held the books at her chest like she was cradling an infant protectively. I took us home as quickly as I had brought her there. I set her down in the dining room where I had once tied and fed her. She looked around for a moment, familiarity in her eyes, before she set the books on the table and smiled.

"Oh, that looks so good," she said.

On the table was a shallow bowl of stew with a mixture of colorful vegetables and the same meat I'd procured for her the following days. Beside that was a purple tinted bread sliced in thick moist slices. It looked quite delicious; I had to admit...but the small tastes of her blood I had gotten so far made the food pale in comparison.

"Sit," I insisted.

Renee did as asked, sitting in a chair I had adjusted so that she could reach the food. I watched her as she ate. There was something sensual about the way she took the spoon in her mouth, licked it clean, and chewed. The way her throat moved when she swallowed lit my desire and I hummed out softly.

She looked at me as I sat down in a chair beside her. Her tongue cleaned her lips, and I ached to touch it.

"You are beautiful even whilst eating," I told her.

She chuckled and bit her bottom lip. Her teeth were blunt and near useless compared to my own, but sharp enough to bring pleasure.

"What doesn't arouse you?" she asked me, her voice lit with teasing.

"Very little," I replied, "with you, I cannot imagine." My eyes trailed from her throat to her toes. "No. Not a thing."

Renee was flush with heat as she continued to eat, and I noted the way she kicked and wiggled her feet occasionally.

"This is so interesting," she said, lifting a half-eaten slice of bread. "It tastes...nothing like the bread I'm used to, but the texture is similar." She squished it in her fingers for a moment and hummed before taking another bite.

"You really are interested in Midaworld, aren't you, Little One?" I asked.

She raised an eyebrow at me. "Of course. I'm not going to live somewhere for...the rest of my life and not know anything about the place. A week ago, I had no idea Midaworld, you, or even Madriel, whatever they are, existed. Now I'm sitting beside you eating...strange but delicious plum colored bread, and a stew made from an animal I do not know of."

I eyed her. "True. You handle that better than most would, you realize."

Renee chewed slowly. "That's a good thing, right?" she asked.

I mused. "Yes. Still, I wonder why."

She swallowed the bite in her mouth before speaking again. "For the same reason that...I'm your mate, I guess. Though, I've always been good at...coping, you could say."

"Humans push a lot of emotion down, but you don't," I told her. "It's what drew me to you."

She nodded, and her brows furrowed. "I used to, though...push it down." She was quiet for a moment, no longer eating. I debated asking her if it had been enough, but she pointed at the books a few feet away on the table. "One of the books Madriel lent me is...not in English. They told me you could read it to me."

Her eyes shifted from the books to me, melting me with affection and interest I had never experienced before. "Will you?"

I stood up and grabbed the book from the table. It was easy to spot, which it was, and I brushed the back of my knuckles along the cover. "Yes. Not tonight. You need to rest, Harvest is soon."

"Alright," Renee replied and slid out of the chair. "Would you at least take me somewhere more comfortable than...your bed for me to read for a bit?" She grabbed the books off the table. I decided to leave the dishes and remaining bread there for now.

"Is it not comfortable?" I asked.

She pursed her lips. "I'm not used to it, it's...a little straining on my body. I'm built differently," she admitted.

I clicked my tongue. "I will remedy that," I told her. "I will require more time and help, it will have to be after Harvest," I stepped closer to her, preparing to scoop her up, but she stepped back.

"I'd like to walk," she said with a smirk. "I have to stretch my legs, you know. After being...tied up."

I purred, the sound vibrating from my chest to my throat. "Yes. You were ravishing in such a position. I will utilize it for the claiming."

Renee squirmed slightly before she started walking, and I could smell it on her arousal, need. Her steps, however, were slightly wider apart than normal, and the wiggle of her hips told me she was sore from earlier.

"Do you remember the way?" I asked, amused. "To the library. It's nothing compared to Madriel's, but the chairs there will be more comfortable."

She shook her head. "I will eventually. Lead the way, my love." She smiled, her nose flushing. It was the first time she had called me such a name. My heart flooded my chest with warmth even hotter than the fire running through my veins.

I led her to the library and brushed off one of the lounge chairs there, lighting several candles with ease. Renee set all but one book down on the ottoman nearby.

"Join me." She reached a hand out to me. I looked at her hand for a moment.

The softness that Renee showed me differed from any relationship I had ever been a part of. Sex and the rough dirty hungry parts of it were so familiar...but this? It was new.

"What?" Renee asked, her eyes suddenly crossed with concern.

I took her hand and sank down in one of the large chairs, and pulled her into my lap. She exhaled in surprise and then settled back against me. The wide curve of her ass in my lap and her soft ringlets of hair just a tilt of my head down were intoxicating.

"There is not much that is new to me, with how long I've lived, but there are many soft things that are," I explained. "I was forged in fire with a hunger for life and darkness. I did not know I could feel...something else."

Renee tilted her head to look up at me, her eyes like the two moons of the Midaworld.

"You've made me feel things I didn't know I could too," she said.

I leaned down and pressed my lips to hers, desperate for a taste of the woman I was unwilling to part with ever. The woman I would soon claim as mine, casting a warning to anyone who thought otherwise.

Renee kissed me back, her mouth sweet and so much smaller. Just as I prodded at her lips with the tip of my tongue, she pulled back.

"Reading and rest, remember," she smirked.

I growled low and brought my lips to her ear, kissing and nipping there. "I will chase you again, someday. I will wear your precious body out until you fall to the floor, too tired to run, and I will taste every inch of you." I pulled back to look into her face.

Her face that was as red as ever. I felt it as she squeezed her thighs together, and her heat radiated on top of me.

"Is that a promise?" she asked.

"And a warning." I bumped her head with my nose and mouth softly, then my cheek. Enjoying the texture of her hair.

She blinked at me, and suddenly giggled, putting a hand to her mouth. Her reaction seeming unexpected.

"What, pet?" I asked.

She cleared her throat. "Nothing," she insisted and waved her hand. "Now, let me read to you."

I eyed her. "First, tell me what this nothing is."

She rolled her eyes. "How about...first, you tell me something about you," she insisted, "what do you do?"

I narrowed my eyes. "What do you mean?"

She chuckled. "Besides chasing down dinner. What do you like to do? Clearly you don't do a lot of reading."

I looked to the side for a moment. "At one point I fought on the front lines," I replied, "it took up much of my time."

"There's war here?" she asked, looking a bit alarmed.

"Not anymore," I told her. "Truthfully... it's been a long while since I have done much other than sate my hunger. Madriel occasionally would drag me out, but I suppose I became more isolated before meeting you."

Renee's brow furrowed. "You had no one before me?" she inquires.

I smirk. "I didn't say that. I have had many lovers. Few became much more."

It was quiet for a moment before I finally spoke again. "Now. Tell me what I asked for."

She sighed, but answered me.

"You...rubbed your face on my head like..." she tilted her head side to side, trailing off, "like Fern does."

My face fell, and I stared at her.

"You asked!" she laughed.

"I will show you I am no house cat," I growled under my breath.

She reached up and caressed my face. "Just let me read to you." She removed her hand and opened the book in her lap.

I settled and allowed myself to relax into the chair, but kept my eyes on her face. She began to read, and at first it was clumsy and her breath was quick as if she was nervous, but after a few moments her voice leveled out.

As she read, she would fidget and shift her position on my lap now and again, and I moved myself to make it more comfortable for her. I watched her fingertips as she turned the pages and admired her small, dainty hands.

Flickers of emotions crossed her eyes every now and again, flitting from her skin into the hair, and I sighed as I pulled it into me. Affection, elation, interest...arousal. Excitement. These tender feelings rising in her from the story she read to me. The words were of little interest to me compared to the rippling haze around her I drank in. The movement of her supple lips and feminine sound of her voice. Still, I paid attention to every detail.

"Are you listening?" she asked at one point.

My eyes were on her mouth. "Yes," I replied, "they are miserable without each other. Isobel is packing to run away."

"Hm." Renee was satisfied with my answer and continued to read.

I watched as tears gathered at the corners of her eyes. Her sadness was such a potent emotion compared to the others. It drew me in closer and I brushed my lips along her ear, then her temple.

"So delicious," I whispered.

She sniffled and looked up at me with teary eyes, stopping in the middle of a sentence. "Does this...feed you?" she asked.

"Mm, yes," I replied. "Surprisingly so." More time than I had expected had passed. She should be resting, but we were still here.

She blinked and her tears dripped down her cheeks. I leaned closer and licked the salty droplets from her skin. One, then another.

Renee leaned up silently and kissed me. I felt her fingers slide onto my jawline and cheek, and hold me to her. I held her tighter with my arm around her waist and kissed her back, slow and deepening.

I slid my tail around her body, snaking it along her hip to her thigh, and brushed the pointed tip along her naked flesh. This provoked a moan from her into my mouth. Every inch of me inside and out yearned for her, still, I pulled back and looked into her eyes.

"Two more sleeps," I told her, "two more, and I will claim you as mine for all to see."

Renee pressed one more soft kiss to my lips. "I can't wait." She looked back down at the book, but didn't continue reading, seeming distracted. Tired.

"It is time to rest," I decided. Though a hungered for more of her flickering emotions.

"Okay, but on one condition," she said.

I growled softly. "Don't test me, Little One." I pressed my tail more firmly against her thigh. Her breath caught, but she didn't waver.

"Tell me what to expect with the ritual," she said. "I know I'll be tied up, like you mentioned, but...I don't want to go in unprepared. You said it can be dangerous. Tell me how." Renee closed the book in her lap, keeping our place with a golden bookmark that had been tucked into the front cover.

I hummed. "Very well, my mate."

14

HARVEST

Renee

"Hold still," Madriel said from behind me. They were securing my dress at the back for what felt like forever. Madriel had wrapped, draped, zipped, and tied me into the many layers of fabric until it was perfectly snug and aligned with my body.

"I'm doing my best," I snapped back. There was a tug on my waist and a chuckle.

"You've got yourself a sassy one here," Madriel commented.

Hale replied from where she sat several feet away. Her crimson eyes were eyeing me hungrily. "I do," she said, "it's part of the fun."

Even with the anxiety crawling up my stomach, I couldn't help but smile.

The dress I wore comprised several types of black fabric that I wasn't completely sure about. If I had to guess, it was tulle, lace, and latex rubber. They adorned every inch from my chest to my mid thighs in the stuff, and what didn't squeeze me fluttered out around me. I looked like an emo teenager's most elaborate paper mache project... It was so unlike anything I would ever, ever worn, but damn, did I look good.

My hair was tied back and braided at the crown. Madriel's smaller fingers were more capable of such a hair style than Hale's. As I stood as still as possible, I gazed at Hale. She had traded her usual leather tube top and hot pants for a cropped leather vest and a short skirt with a slit at either side. It was undoubtedly less complicated than my attire, but equally sexy. I swallowed my desire, knowing that it wouldn't be long before I'd get more than my fill of pleasure.

Hale had filled me in on most of the details of the ritual, and I hadn't been able to stop thinking about it. Knowing that soon I would be surrounded by other creatures who would be watching as I bared it all to Hale was both nerve-wracking and exhilarating.

"There, now you're ready." Madriel stepped in front of me and drew their eyes around my body, up and down. They smiled in satisfaction. "Absolutely stunning. They are going to eat you up."

Hale stepped closer and brushed the back of her knuckle against my cleavage where the lace was. It spread across my breasts and stopped just underneath them, my nipples partially visible through the several layers of ornate lace. "But I'll be the only one tasting."

My face flushed, and I stepped down from the stool I was standing on.

Madriel tsked Hale. "No touching until the ritual. The dress must be perfect."

A low rumble came from Hale. "Soon," she promised me, looking down into my eyes. I was wet just thinking about it. I forced myself to look away from her and over to Madriel.

They were dressed elegantly in black and purples that brushed the ground with each step, even with the tall heels they had on. "Well, I have some things to attend to before the Harvest, so I will see you two there," Madriel wiggled their fingers.

"Thank you for...this," I smiled and motioned at myself.

"Damn right, thank you," Madriel replied, "you owe me one, Hale." They smirked.

Before I could even wonder how Hale would pay Madriel back, they had disappeared from the room.

Hale's face came to meet my neck, her tongue glided up the side of my throat. I shivered and closed my eyes.

"I would claim you right now if I could," she said under her breath.

I bit my lip. "Don't tease me." My gaze screamed *'no please continue'.*

Hale's breath was hot against my neck, and all I could do was close my eyes. I just reveled in the feeling for a moment or two until she backed away from me. She lifted the vile that Madriel had brought several days before up in front of me.

"Drink this, it's part of the ritual to connect us," she told me. Wolfsbane, I remembered.

I eyed the vile of swirling purple liquid before taking it and uncorking it. I tilted it to my lips.

"All of it."

It was tart and far too bitter on my tongue and small pieces of plant matter made the texture rather unpleasant. Still, I swallowed it down until it was gone. I handed the vile back and it was set down nearby.

I felt a slight shiver up my spine.

"Do we need to get going yet?" I asked. "Where is...the Harvest taking place?" I had yet to actually be outside in the Midaworld yet. See more than the peaks out of windows gave me. The red glow of the sun was almost as beautiful as the purple and orange colors that made up the night. I wanted to see more.

"Not far," Hale replied. "I will be carrying you. Unless you'd like to fight that." She narrowed her eyes at me with a slight smirk on her face.

I folded my arms under my bust and stepped closer. "And if I would?" I asked.

Hale leaned down and brushed her forehead against mine. "Then I would warn you that you need to save your energy."

I lifted a hand and pressed my fingers to her lips. "Mm. Fine. This time I won't put up a fight," I smiled at her.

With that, Hale swept me off my feet as she had so many times already. I was positive that I'd never grow tired of feeling her arms underneath me, holding me tightly to her chest and feeling her warmth surround me.

I felt excitement bubble up inside me as I realized I was being taken outside. The largest wooden door opened up, and I was carried down stone stairs and out into the open air. The air was hotter outside, but fresher, and a breeze played with my hair. Tall, dark trees with empty twisting branches grew on either side of a cobbled path. The night sky was pitch darkness intermingling with specks of purple and orange. As my eyes found the moon, full and bright, it found another nearby. Their faded colors opposite of each other, one orange and the other navy blue.

I hardly said a word as she carried me. Even once we moved at a speed beyond my ability to see much around us, I took in what I could. The passing blurs of stone and wooden houses, flickering lights and signs in a language that I wouldn't understand, anyway.

Finally, Hale slowed, and I was carried down the stairs and into a large building. As we entered a dimly lit ballroom with glowing chandeliers, the sound of chatter and laughter filled my ears.

Hale set me down on my feet, but I did not move far. I knew what was to come first.

I could feel eyes on me, some glowing and others void of any light or color, as Hale secured a metal collar around my neck. The inside padded lightly with leather, but the outside was pristinely polished. At the center was a lock that was clicked shut, and a loop for the leash to be fed through. I tilted my chin up, so that it was easy for Hale to do so. Her claws wrapped around the end of the leash.

"Good Girl," Hale said, quietly, just for my eyes, but I knew others heard it. "How does it feel?"

My neck was tingling. I'd worn chokers and necklaces before, but this was different. The metal was stiff and restricting, but the control I gave away and trusted Hale with was freeing.

"Good," I replied simply.

Hale led me forward, tugging just enough to make it clear where she wanted me, but not so harsh as to literally drag me along. I was a willing pet, and based on the curious eyes of the other creatures around us, that was beyond intriguing to them.

I paid attention to where Hale was leading me as best as possible while also taking in my surroundings. Beings with large wings and horns. Others with multiple eyes and teeth that jutted out from the bottom of their lips. So many colors, dark and dusty in their ways and others were lighter, almost pastel. There were so many people to take in, I could hardly process it all. Desperate to know just who and what the creature with seemingly no nose and ears shaped like butterflies was.

"Hale," a deep voice spoke, and my gaze wandered over. Hale gripped the leash tighter. They continued to speak in a language I didn't understand.

"I rarely miss Harvest," Hale said.

I wondered if I should step closer, uncertain who this person was.

All around us people were drinking, dancing and some even making out. I struggled to decide where to even look until Hale spoke once more and I drew my attention to the being before us.

"This is Renee," Hale introduced me, "I will be claiming her tonight." Hale looked down at me. "Renee, this is Karvok."

My eyes shifted back to Karvok. They were just as tall as Hale with skin the color and transparency of honey. I could see black veins snaking along their face and neck, as well as their hands when they waved them to talk. They met my eyes with their own completely black ones.

"How delectable she is," Karvok said this time in English, "...and how exciting. We've not seen a human be claimed in over a decade."

I tilted my head, ignoring the burning desire to get on with the ritual already. I knew Hale would lead me where I needed to be when it was time.

"Oh, how cute," another voice, another person, approached. "I'd love a taste before she's claimed." They flashed their fangs. My body stiffened, and I shifted closer to Hale. This made the recent addition and Karvok laugh.

"She's mine. Only I will taste her," Hale replied, stern and confident.

My shoulders relaxed some.

I watched as the one who wanted to taste me sipped from a glass of thick red liquid. There was a powerful scent of iron in the room, so I didn't have to imagine what many of the guests were drinking.

Many others approached us, and they took me in with their eyes and senses as though I was a forbidden snack, and I quickly realized that I was just that. Hale kept me close by, leading me with the leash as she made her way about, mingling. She occasionally spoke in that tongue I couldn't understand, but I noticed the way she urged others to speak so that I would. Many of their accents were thick, and it was clear they were not used to speaking in my language.

Ignoring the anxiety that spread through me at having so many eyes on me and mouths that wished to devour me hovering close by, I mused to myself. Wondering just how long it would take if I tried to learn this new language. I had picked up Spanish fairly quickly in grade school and could still wiggle my way around a conversation, but...a language I had never heard of...that would surely be more difficult.

"She's so well behaved," someone said, drawing my attention back. I bristled at the comment, and my face showed it.

"Oh, I think she didn't like that."

My fingers curled against my dress. "I can bite too," I replied. Tired of being silent and reserved.

Hale tugged on the leash, and I thought it was in disapproval at first before she said, "I wouldn't underestimate my Little One."

I flushed happily. "I did come back to her, after all."

The creature's eyes flicked around to each other curiously and then to Hale.

"She means she stayed willingly," Hale corrects me and shoots me a quick glance. I realize she doesn't want the others to know she let me go. I should have known that. I bite the inside of my cheek. Maybe being quiet is good.

"Wow, brave little thing," one of them says. "I wonder how long she'll last."

My brow furrowed. "Forever." I insisted. How long was forever here? I wasn't even sure if I aged normally.

Another chuckled darkly. "They all think that. Madriel's did."

I blinked and looked to Hale, whose eyes darkened. "You know better," Hale said.

They tsked. "Please. It's been long enough."

Suddenly there Madriel was, long legs and flowing hair outshining almost everyone in the room. They spat something in that infernal tongue and the others hissed and rolled their eyes before disappearing into the crowd.

"Those fuckers can find something better to do," Madriel snipped before standing in front of us. They looked me up and down. "Hm, ravishing yes. I knew it would match the collar."

My ears heated, but I found myself relieved it was just Madriel now.

"She's a vision," Hale agreed and gripped the leash tighter, forcing me to nearly rub up against her. I tilted my head and brushed my forehead against her arm, enjoying the heat of her closeness.

"Are you staying?" I asked Madriel, feeling more comfortable talking.

They scoffed and tilted a glass to their lips. "I have my reservations about this whole thing, but I'm sure as hell not going to miss seeing my artistry in action." They licked their lips and looked to the side. "Warning, Valiri is headed this way, and she looks awfully hungry."

Madriel smirked.

Hale growled in irritation. "She always is."

"Would you like me to hold your pet?" Madriel asked and extended one of their slender manicured hands.

Hale seemed to struggle with the decision, tugging me closer for a moment.

"Oh, come on, I won't bite them...but you know she might," Madriel said.

"Dammit," Hale grumbled. She looked down at me. "Only a moment." She slowly handed the end of the leash to Madriel.

My pulse picked up, and I looked at Madriel, who was grinning in far too much amusement for my comfort. I swallowed hard. "I'm following you, you're not leading me." I insisted. "This is for Hale." I was not *Madriel's* pet.

"Oh, hush, come on girl," Madriel said with a slightly sweeter tone at the end and clicked their tongue at me. My face was red, but I didn't stop my feet from moving and doing as they asked. I glared at them the entire time, though.

We stopped some yards away from where Hale stood, and I could now see this Valiri that was approaching. Her skin was a mixture of darkest night and fuzzy gray, she glittered in the lighting, and her spider eyes blinked at different rates. Several arms gutted out from her sides, one of which was holding a glass.

My core tightened as I watched another one of those hands brush Hale's arm.

"Who is she?" I asked.

"A former lover," Madriel replied casually.

Jealousy boiled in my stomach. "Hale's ex?"

They laughed. "Yes. On and off for...hells, quite a while—but they've not enjoyed each other in some time," they said. Their gaze shifted down to me. I noticed they held the leash loosely now, not forcing me in any direction.

"Should I be worried?" I asked, genuinely. An ache in my stomach as I watched. Hale seemed...reserved, not very interested in whatever they were talking about.

Madriel looked at me with a cocked brow. "It's you she's claiming...so I think not," Madriel replied, "...Valiri, however, she could pose an issue. Nothing Hale can't handle, hopefully." They took another drink.

I grew more irritated that I wasn't over there hearing them speak. Maybe they weren't even talking in English.

The tension in the room grew as if felt like seconds and minutes blended into one.

"You know, I never thanked you for getting some things for Fern," I said to Madriel, trying to distract myself.

"It's nothing. When Hale told me you actually brought your cat with you, "Madriel chuckled, "well, I have to admit I was quite amused. Fern must be very special, so I couldn't let her go without the necessities."

I smiled softly. I could tell Madriel was being nonchalant. "And a few toys."

"The necessities, as I said."

Finally, Hale made her way over to me, Valiri following behind. She took the leash from Madriel and tugged me close. The collar felt like a comfortable arm holding me, letting me know she was there and I was hers.

"Renee is this Valiri," Hale said. "Valiri, as mentioned, this is Renee."

Valiri eyed me, and a fake look of interest crossed her face, a gentle smile. "Pleasure to meet the one being claimed this evening."

I stayed quiet.

"Naughty pet," Valiri scolded and looked to Hale. "I'd be such a better one."

I gritted my teeth.

"Zarkov is looking," Hale said, voice low, "I'm sure he'd be interested."

Valiri glared. "As if," she huffed. She looked at me, and I glared back at her. "Find me when your little human can't handle the ritual."

With that, she stormed off, and Madriel snickered from beside us.

"I love seeing her jealous," they said. "Both of them, really."

Hale leaned down and brushed their lips against mine. My body stilled. I knew we weren't supposed to kiss again until the ritual, but I wanted to so badly.

Hale stopped before it became a genuine kiss, but slid her mouth up to whisper in my ear.

"You have nothing to worry about, Little One."

Hale led me to the center of the room by the leash and up a few stairs onto a platform that was risen at least six feet from the floor. There were various anchor points and chains lined up around, and just the sight of them made goosebumps crawl up my back. I wasn't led to any of them however, no I was led to the center of the stage where several ropes were let down from above.

Hale removed the leash from the collar but left the collar on.

"Keep your eyes on me," she whispered as she leaned down.

I nodded and locked eyes with her. "Yes, Mistress." My knees were already weak, but with more than just interest. I knew if I looked around, there would be dozens of eyes on me, and my pulse quickened at the thought. I did as she asked, keeping my eyes on her, even when I couldn't meet her gaze anymore.

Hale secured the ropes around my wrists tighter and tighter until I was forced to stand on my tiptoes. My mind flickered back to that first moment I had woken up in the dark room, dangling from the ceiling.

I took a deep breath and let the tension take me, allowing my anxious mind to settle into the comfortable pull and gentle sway of my suspended body. The other eyes in the room didn't matter. Their murmurs of desire and interest were a lull in the background. I knew what to say if it all became too much, and I trusted her.

I kept my attention on Hale, who was running her claws along the back of the dress. I could hear the fabric rip and pop.

I squirmed beneath her touch as it slid to the front of my body. Her head tilted down and her teeth sunk into the small holes of the lace and pulled. The lace tore from the bodice and revealed my bare breasts. Heat swelled up from my stomach along my collarbones and neck.

"So beautiful," Hale purred. I swooned.

The tip of her claws tucked into the dress along my ribs and sliced the fabric with ease. Her monstrous hands and teeth tore and destroyed each carefully secured strip and sewn piece. I shivered as her teeth grazed the tops of my thighs.

Madriel had so expertly crafted the dress in a way I didn't realize until then. Rather than one piece that could be torn and removed quickly, it was many pieces that came together and allowed Hale to unwrap me like a present.

Just a few soft pieces of velvet were left, they clung to my hips and groin so delicately. Hale's nose and mouth brushed against my pussy through the fabric, and my back arched. I was so flushed now. Covered in blotchy pink patches from head to toe.

I felt and heard Hale inhale and growl low. I felt the vibration against my clit and my breath hitched. I wanted to close my eyes and lean my head back, but I kept my eyes on her.

Hale's tongue dipped into the band of the makeshift panties just enough for her to ease the velvet into her mouth and she tore them from my body with her teeth.

The tattered pieces of the dress were scattered about, and I was left completely naked before her and the hungry spectators. The air in the room was beyond thick.

Her hand slipped between my thighs and I felt something round and smooth slide along my pussy, collecting my already wet arousal there. It was cold at first, but as she slid it thrice, it warmed and my need grew.

I gasped as she slid the egg sized object inside of my pussy, and my walls clenched softly.

"Hale," I whimpered as my breath grew heavier.

I wanted her close to me, touching and tasting every part, but she moved back. I knew this would happen, but it still filled me with impatience.

I watched as Hale knelt on the stage several yards from me. A masked figure came up the stairs and approached her. They secured the chains at her sides to her waist, ankles, and wrists. Something emanated from those chains, glowing a low and ominous red.

The masked person exited the stage as quickly as they had arrived, and the crowd was buzzing.

Hale's eyes met mine, and suddenly the egg inside of me began to vibrate. Electricity shot down into my toes and they stiffened against the edge of the floor. It was not Hale who was controlling it; I knew that much, but it didn't matter.

My hips twitched, and I squirmed against the pleasure that rattled from inside, squeezing my thighs together. "Oh-Ah." A gasp stuck in my throat.

Hale's brilliant crimson eyes glowed brighter, and her demeanor grew restless. She tugged against the chains.

I kept myself locked on her, even as the vibration grew more intense and my eyes begged me to close them. My chest rose with my uneven breaths. I wiggled against my bindings, wanting so desperately to touch myself, but I couldn't. I could only writhe against the vibrating egg buried in my cunt as I began to drip with arousal.

Hale's eyes fell to my pussy at that moment, and her tongue practically lolled out of her mouth. She growled and tugged against the chains once more, harder, and I could hear them creaking.

"H-Hale I..." I groaned. The pressure was building up so high in my core. The muscles in my thighs tensed and I panted softly, trying my best not to give in, but my legs were shaking.

Hale's eyes burned with raw, intense need, and she appeared in that moment even bigger than she was. Her muscles strained and flexed as she pulled at the chains and shackles. I watched as her body twitched, as she panted and growled in absolute primal desire. Every ounce of humanity had been pushed to the wayside, and she was snarling and snapping at the edges of her sanity.

It was that look of the animal that sent me tumbling over the edge of my orgasm.

I cried out as my pussy squeezed and dripped around the furiously vibrating egg. My thighs, coated in my juices, shivered and ached.

It seemed my coming undone was the catalyst for Hale's freedom, as she ripped herself free from the chains, shackles still clinging to her wrists and ankles. She bolted for me faster than I could see, a growling blur of teeth, horns, and claws before me.

I yelped as her hands grabbed my thighs and her claws sunk into my tender flesh, so much deeper than before. The pain shot up my back and I couldn't help but screw my eyes shut. Her mouth found my pussy before I could even process the pain, and her long forked tongue thrust inside of me, curling around the egg and pulling it out. I heard it clank against the stage and suddenly she was inside of me again.

My legs were over her broad shoulders as she filled me with her tongue and her claws scratched and tore my skin. I bucked up against her face as pleasure coursed through me. Tears licked at my eyes as an equal measure of pain flooded me. Blood dripped down my legs.

"M-Mistress," I cried, "Hale! Fuck!"

I pulled at the ropes binding my hands, burning, aching, desperate to grab her and hold on to her hair and horns; but I couldn't.

As my orgasm found me, it was too much. My hips thrashed and bucked against her face. My lips quivered as I moaned and grasped. My pussy was so sensitive that just her nose pressing against my clit made me whine desperately.

"Mine!" Hale growled, her voice barely coherent.

I cried out as her teeth sunk into the inside of my thigh. Her tongue licked and swirled as she drank headily from me. Fire crawled up my leg and into my stomach and the tears that had been sitting on the edge of my waterline finally dripped down my cheeks.

I felt one of her hands move up my body to my tits, and she caressed and squeezed one of them. Her fingers caught my hardening nipple and tugged just hard enough to make the other tingle in phantom pain and pleasure.

Hale's teeth pulled from me, bloody and sharp. My entire body twitched and shivered as I struggled to distinguish pain from pleasure, desire from terror; but as she stood towering above me and ripped the rope from my wrists... I realized it was all the above.

I was terrified, and I had never been more aroused in my life.

15

CLAIMED

Hale

Blood. So thick and delicious. Iron and honey. My perfect girl. My perfect beautiful Little One. The taste of her blood and cum in my vicious mouth. I could think of nothing else. I could smell nothing else.

The world around me did not exist. Only the cries of pleasure and pain from the woman I claimed. My claws cut the rope, and I had her on the floor.

My clothing was gone in the blink of an eye.

Needy, greedy...hungry. So hungry. I drank in her aura, bursting and exploding with emotion in quick, desperate pulls of my own. It filled me with a passion so overwhelming that I groaned into the crook of Renee's shoulder.

Everything moved quick and hard. My red naked body pressed down against her tanned one as I rocked between her wet bloody thighs, my clit against hers, then pressed inside of her, shallow and throbbing.

She moaned breathlessly underneath me, her face and body twisting with her pleasure that soaked into my own and created an intoxicating scent. She grabbed at me needily, at my fur and my skin, as I rocked my hips into hers.

I leaned my head down and took her nipple in my mouth, sucking and swirling my tongue around the hard, sensitive nub. My hand palmed the other.

"Hale!" Renee cried, her face dripping with tears. Her nails dug into my back, pushing and scratching against my skin desperately.

"Mine, mine...mine!" I growled and fucked her harder, faster. A tight bubble of pleasure rose inside of me.

I bit down into her throat, and her blood flooded my mouth.

So good.

So...much.

I bit her again on her shoulder. Then her arm. Again and again. Losing myself to the thirst. Her taste was so potent on my tongue.

I couldn't take too much. It was time to give her mine. To complete the ritual. But I wanted more. More. More. More!

I was kissing her; I didn't know for how long. I growled into her mouth and she whimpered into mine.

I reached to my shoulder and ripped myself open with my claws, letting my hot black blood drip out of me.

"Drink," I huffed and grabbed Renee's head. Her eyes were all but rolled back.

She moaned, barely able to move her head, but then her mouth was on the slashes, sucking and licking at my blood. Her hands grabbed my horns and gripped tightly.

Everything was hazy.

I felt it happen. The rush of emotion from my toes and up my ass to my head as we became one. As my dark soul twisted with hers and everything else in the universe ceased to matter.

I could feel Renee writhe and cum beneath me, again, and again, but I was seeing from her eyes. I could see the horror of my face, glistening bloody teeth and piercing eyes. The monster filled with hunger and desire that was overtaking her and claiming her. I felt her emotions clearer than ever. Arousal, fear, need, love...exhaustion.

Her head fell from my shoulder, her face and neck smeared with my blood. I saw her instead of me again. She reached for me with shaky hands and somehow I knew exactly what she wanted.

I kissed her hard and feral. My teeth cut her lips and the tip of her tongue, but she did not pull from me. She kissed me back, moaning and panting my name again and again.

"I'm yours," Renee whispered.

As my pleasure found me again, rippling along my thighs and cunt, I began to find myself. Easing down from the carnal need to rip her limb from limb and drink until there was nothing left. A feat I had never accomplished until now.

My mind was drunk with pleasure and soaked in a heady wave of blood lust. My vision was dark around the edges, zoning in on one person and one person only. Renee. I could taste her blood in my mouth still, iron and honey on my tongue. It was still sticky on my chin and glistening on the points of my teeth.

All I could see, hear, taste and smell was Renee in my arms. My legs carried me back home on autopilot. I didn't remember even picking her up from the stage and moving. The only thing that mattered in that moment was the flood of pure ecstasy that came from our unholy bond, and getting Renee somewhere safe.

The others at Harvest had already started to disappear into their own nights of pleasure, feeding, and debauchery. Turned on by the claiming ritual, they had been so lucky to see.

It was only 3/4ths of the way home that I realized my house was not the best place to take her. Madriel would have the things needed to take care of Renee's wounds, even as limited as they were. I gained enough control over myself to switch my tracks to go to Madriel's instead.

Renee whined softly in my arms, her body curling up against me and her fingers were gripping the fur at my shoulders. Her wounds were no longer dripping, thanks to my blood she had ingested, but she was far from being healed.

The closer I got to Madriel's, the weaker I felt. The adrenaline of the ritual was leaving me and I was running on fumes. I knew Madriel would not be home, but surely it would still be better for her there. Better for us there.

Everything grew hazy again, and that focus of vision on Renee was becoming more akin to not being able to see at all. I stumbled into the foyer and down the corridor, turning into the first room I found.

Renee was growing cold in my arms, and her sounds became less and less.

She had to survive this; she was strong enough; I knew she was.

I cursed to myself as I grew woozy, unable to stand. Holding her in my lap on the floor, I reached for the nearest blanket in the ornate guest bedroom I was in. I paid no attention to anything besides wrapping Renee in the thick blanket until all but her face was covered. I slumped to the floor with her in my arms.

"Little One," I whispered. "Stay with me."

I bit into my palm and then pressed it to her mouth. Her lips parted, and she licked at the blood on my skin in small kitten licks.

"Good Girl," I hummed, and let everything go fuzzy.

"Oh, fucking hell," Madriel said from above us. "That's a perfectly good duvet your pet is bleeding onto."

I opened my eyes, not sure when they'd closed, to see Madriel glaring at me from where they stood. Their face was covered in blood and viscera, and their eyelids were half open as they stood blood drunk.

"Here is better," I replied simply. Struggling to find my words. "Safe."

Madriel licked their lips and brushed their hair was a sweaty forehead. "Up, she needs more than a blanket and your blood."

I struggled to get up, feeling heavier than I had ever felt in my entire life.

"Fuck me," Madriel exhaled. Their eyes shifted to Renee's face, also covered in blood, peaking out of the blanket, and suddenly softened. "Let me have her."

My pulse quickened, and I couldn't help the hiss that escaped me as I gripped her tighter.

Madriel leaned down. "Hush, darling. I'm going to help you," they insisted. "You're in no condition." Madriel brushed my hair, matted with blood, from my face.

"Thank you," I whispered, barely recognizing my voice.

Madriel pulled Renee from the blanket and into their arms. I saw then the extent of her injuries. Her naked body was covered in bite marks and bruises had already formed at her softest points. A sense of pride and affection rippled along my blackened heart. I wished to kiss each one, but for now, I would let Madriel tend to her.

16

THE ONE WITH AFTER CARE

Renee

I was sitting on a porch swing. The breeze was warm and smelled of freshly baked goods. I could hear children playing in the background, and I sensed I was one myself, but I didn't get up to play with them. I tucked my knees up under a cozy flannel blanket and opened up a book I had read dozens of times already.

A love story. My grandmother said I was too young for such things, but my mother continued to buy them for me and insist it was good for my soul. So, nana let me read them. Even when I was staying at her house.

"I'd rather see you reading than making a mess," Nana would tell me. "Just don't go letting any of these boys try to kiss you. You're too young for kisses. Much too young for that."

I would simply blush and continue reading.

My hands were small, so were my feet, and I was still at that stage of my preteen fashion sense where I wore brightly colored leggings under all of my clothing. They peaked out from my denim skirt, and up from my brown boots, and assured me I'd be warm and comfortable. When I touched my lip, I felt no scar there. So I hadn't yet tried and failed to get my lip pierced at a sleepover.

All of this told me I was twelve years old, and it was the autumn that I realized it wasn't just boys I liked.

It was the year my father caught me kissing another girl in nana's garden.

It was the year my father stopped meeting my gaze when he spoke to me.

It was the year he stopped joining me to the park in the summer.

And it was the year that nana told me she loved me, no matter what.

I gasped as my eyes opened. The last thing I remembered was Hale on top of me, and her blood filling my mouth. I could still taste it. Like charcoal and rosewater. It lingered on my tongue and created a sticky film on my face.

I felt arms underneath me, equally strong as Hale's, but slender and colder where they touched me.

My breath left me as my vision cleared and I saw Madriel, and realized that they were the one carrying me.

"Hale," I choked out.

"It's alright," Madriel insisted, voice quiet. "Hale is resting."

I was too tired to fight, so I simply let my body relax into their arms. I gazed at the face from below, seeing the blood and bit and pieces of god only knew clinging there. They looked different. Not so put together and calm. Their eyes swirled with golden and silver, burning more brightly than before. They must have just gotten back from hunting, I mused.

We were in Madriel's home, this I knew instantly from the decor. I wasn't sure why, but I didn't question it.

Every part of me ached and stung, even with how gentle Madriel was as they carried me. Between my legs was sore and sensitive. Just the slightest shift of my thighs made my stomach tense.

"Is she...okay?" I asked about Hale.

Madriel turned into a room, and with a flick of their wrists, it lit up. "She will be," they replied. "It's you who needs tending to."

I licked my lips, thirsty...so thirsty, but I couldn't seem to voice that.

As they shifted me in their arms, I realized I was naked, but it didn't bother me like I expected. After all, Madriel had just seen everything Hale had done to me, as had countless others. Being naked seemed...tame, in comparison.

I heard water running, though they did not touch the bath that sat in the corner of the room. It was larger than even Hale's and was a corner bath with gently rumbling jets on all sides.

I was quiet until they placed me in the bath. I hissed and groaned at the hot water touching my skin and wounds. I brushed my fingers along my neck, touching them...my shoulder. My arm. It almost appeared there was not an inch of my body that Hale had not marked.

This stirred something dark and wanton inside of me. I sunk more relaxed into the bath after a moment and leaned my head back, closing my eyes.

The water stopped running once it reached my breasts. I heard some gentle sloshing and then felt something soft on my shoulder. I opened my eyes and realized Madriel was bathing me.

My ears heated, and my pulse quickened. "I-I can do that," I insisted and reached for the cloth. I felt taken aback by the fact that they would even try, that they would even be comfortable with that.

"Very well," they replied, and let me take the sudsy cloth for myself.

My brow furrowed, but I continued where they had started, gently washing my shoulders and neck, ignoring the pain as I did so.

My eyes drifted over and I watched as Madriel sat at the edge of the tub and reached in, collecting water and soap on their fingers and then washing their face.

They didn't seem...as bothered by this as I expected. They were complaining, nor were they glaring at me.

I looked away before they looked at me and continued to bathe, slow and gentle. My head felt as heavy as a rock, but I kept it up.

After cleaning their face, Madriel left my side for just a moment before returning with a vial. They opened it and held it to my lips.

"Drink," they ordered.

I touched their hand with mine as I did as I was told and drank down the antiseptic flavored green liquid that left a slight numbness on my tongue.

"Why are you doing this?" I asked. My voice was just a whisper.

Madriel closed the vial and tapped one of their fingers on the top. They were quiet as they stepped closer and sat on the edge of the tub again.

"I've known Hale for many years," they explained, "I never thought Hale would claim a human, much less...fall in love with one."

My heart fluttered in my chest. I hadn't said that word yet. Neither had Hale. To myself or her, or anyone really; but I knew it as I sat bathing away the aches and pains of a ritual more intense than any human wedding could be... that I loved her.

I looked down and away from Madriel, feeling vulnerable, despite everything I had been through.

As I bathed, I thought about what Madriel had said days before.

You know how this ended for me.

About what they said about Madriel at the ritual.

I turned to look at them hesitantly. "We're you in love with a human before?" I asked.

Madriel went rigid for a moment and simply stared at me. "Yes," they said as they relaxed.

I looked at them expectantly, wanting to know more but being too anxious to voice that. It was silent for so long that I thought the topic had been closed, so I looked back at the water, but then they spoke again.

"Semi-human, my mate was at least," Madriel said. "I claimed him as my own during a time of...incredibly greed and struggle in the Midaworld."

I pulled my knees close to myself, ignoring the ache, and listened.

"He was killed by a pair of retched slugs that wanted him for themselves," they told me and my heart clenched.

"I'm sorry," I whispered.

Madriel tilted their head, their face rather void of emotion for what they were talking about. "I made a mistake," they replied, "...I thought I could keep him safe. I was wrong."

They stood from the edge of the tub. "I only hope you don't suffer the same fate."

I wrapped my arms around myself, tears burning at my waterline. Any response I might have had was stuck in my throat.

"Thank you for telling me," I finally said.

Madriel nodded.

Just in that moment, the door opened and Hale slowly walked in, looking much less worse for wear than I did physically. However, her eyes were tired and across one of her shoulders were several sticky healing slashes. I vaguely remembered licking her blood from them and feeling it drip down my throat. I lifted a hand to my lips, touching them for a moment.

"How is she?" Hale asked, glancing at Madriel.

Madriel stepped to the doorway. "Why don't you ask her yourself?" they suggested and motioned to me. Their voice was calm and level. "I gave her a potion, she should heal much faster, but she should take it easy for a while."

I looked away from Madriel and back to Hale. I wasn't sure how long "a while" was, but based on how utterly sore and torn up I was still, I could guess it wasn't just a day or two.

Hale stepped over to me and knelt at the bath by my side. "How are you feeling?" she asked.

I smiled softly and reached a hand out, brushing my fingers along her cheek. Her mouth and chin were coated in my blood, sticky and coagulating. "I'm okay," I insisted.

I felt something pull in my chest with her nearby. A fuzzy warmth that almost spread outward beyond my body and connected to her. There was something else there, too. Something I couldn't put my finger on, but the first image in my mind was that of a glittering piece of string tied between us.

"And you?" I asked.

Hale leaned forward and pressed her lips to mine. The taste of my blood flecked off into my mouth, but I didn't cringe away. I let it dissolve until all I could taste was her kiss. It lasted for only a moment, much too short, but I was too tired to lean in for more as she pulled away.

"I am yours as you are mine," Hale replied, "...in that I am better than I could ever be."

My fingers curled against her face, and I could hardly handle the affection I felt at that moment. My eyes stung with tears. I looked to the side behind her and noticed Madriel was no longer in the room, having left to give us privacy.

"Join me?" I asked. Hale's face shifted in uncertainty, so I added. "Nothing smutty, I promise. I just want you to hold me."

Hale brushed my hair behind my ear and nodded. I watched as she stood, naked, and stepped into the bath. She sunk into the water, rising the level just enough to cause some of it to drip off the side and onto the tile, but not completely flood the floor.

We said nothing as she reached for me and pulled me gently into her chest, and held me until the water got cold. Then, I was pulled from the bath, dried off in tender motions, and fed... fed until my stomach was full and I was sated.

17

HUNGER

Renee

Over the next few days, I was essentially bed and chair bound. Despite the elixir Madriel had given me, I was still sore and aching from head to toe. I was utterly exhausted even after sleeping for most of the time, but Hale didn't seem to mind.

With Madriel's help, Hale acquired a bed more suited to me and stayed by my side as I rested. Fern was equally stuck to me those days. Lying on my stomach and chest, licking at my wounds that were visible and expressing her own concern by insisting that she eat right beside me.

I had gotten a better grasp on the days in the Midaworld, how long they were, and when each started. So I knew it was the fourth day that I woke up feeling as though I had actually rested. My head was clearer and I could roll over to sleep on any side without flinching.

That morning, I sat up in bed eating the food Hale had brought to me. "You know, I'm not the worst cook in the world," I said, "I'd like to attempt something sometime."

Hale sat on the edge of the bed beside me, and Fern was tucked under the blanket near my legs, kneading at the mattress. "I suppose that can be arranged," she replied.

I smiled and took another bite of bread, enjoying the soft inside and slightly crispy outside. I continued eating in silence for another moment before I found myself gazing at my arm. I could still see the scabbing healing puncture wounds in my flesh.

"Will any of these leave scars?" I asked, curious.

Hale's eyes darted about my body, that was covered in only a short black nightgown. She leaned closer and brushed my curls behind my shoulder, revealing more of my neck and shoulder. "This one might," she told me and ran her knuckles along the bite on my shoulder. "The shoulder scars more easily."

I pursed my lips and looked down at it.

"Are you bothered by it?" she asked me.

I looked up into her eyes, my eyebrows lifted. "No," I insisted. I looked back down and found my face flushing. "...I actually might like it a little." I murmured.

Hale turned my chin with her finger, making me look up at her. She kissed me despite the taste of food in my mouth, just for a second, and pulled away. Her eyes flickered with hunger, and it was as though I could truly feel it flutter from her to me in the air.

"You like my marks on you?" she asked.

"Yes," I replied with certainty. Butterflies zooming around in my stomach. "I do."

Hale purred and leaned back from me.

"Though, perhaps the ones that leave scars should be saved for special occasions," I suggested. "I'm rather tired of being in this bed."

She nodded. "Mm. Yes. Not devouring you whole took much energy from me as well. I prefer to play with you less rough."

My thighs flushed. I set the empty bowl and wooden spoon to the side of me and scooted closer to her. "Just a little less rough?" I asked playfully. I ran my fingers along my collarbones.

Hale exhaled and closed her eyes as she replied. "Just rough enough," she said, and slowly opened her eyes as though returning from a fantasy.

I bit my lip and held her eyes, enjoying the intensity there. "What were you thinking about?" I asked.

Her forked tongue peaked out for a moment, crossing over her lips before disappearing. "I shouldn't say," she told me, "less I...work myself up."

I frowned. "You've hardly touched me the last few days," I said. "I know why, I'm healing...but..." I shifted up onto my knees and wiggled close to her, ignoring my aching muscles. "Even with how sore I am,God, I want you all the time." I laughed, my face pink. "Is that part of our...bond?" I squinted.

Hale's arms wrapped around me and pulled me closer, tighter than she had allowed herself to the last days, but she still kept our chests apart. "Perhaps," she answered. "I feel it too, but I never did not."

I wrapped my arms around her neck as I climbed into her lap and straddled her. Fern peaked up and looked at us for just a moment before returning to her kneading.

"Well, you couldn't possibly scar me more," I said teasingly.

Hale growled low. "Won't. My ability, however," she narrowed her eyes, and I knew what she meant. She could end me.

I chuckled weakly and shook my head. "I trust you," I insisted. "...besides, I consented to these." I brushed my fingers along my other arm, feeling the rough, healing skin. "I've had some close calls with ones I didn't. Thankfully, they healed." I felt my stomach tense. I hadn't intended to bring that up.

Hale eyed my face, her own expression darkening. "Who?" she asked.

I shook my head. "It's over. My life there is over, so that doesn't matter anymore. Right?" I asked, mostly myself. I sunk closer against her, and felt her hand brush my back, up and down.

"Being here does not erase your life there," she said simply. "Tell me. Who hurt you? The man who broke your heart?"

I swallowed thickly and shook my head again. "It's...nothing," I tried to insist and shifted on her lap, but she held me still and just looked at me until the words were burning to get out of my mouth. "My father," I explained. "...he wasn't the nicest man growing up."

Hale's jaw tightened. "I remember you said you might miss fighting with him."

I sighed and looked away from her. "As an adult our fighting is, was, mostly just ridiculous shit. He never touched me once I was grown. As a kid though, especially when he was struggling with work, he...could be a serious bastard." I shook my head and looked at her.

Hale had a wicked look in her eyes. "He will never hurt you again," she told me. "In any way."

I furrowed my brow. "I know. I'm here now," I agreed.

I leaned close and rubbed my nose against hers, then pulled back to just look at her. She was so...hot, in more ways than one. Her body close to mine was comfortable and eased some of my pain.

I groaned and tilted my head back. "Ugh. I was trying to be sexy and ended up talking about my fucking trauma instead. Fuck." I laughed in the middle of my groan and tilted my head back up. My pulse pounded near my temples and I cringed.

Hale's claws brushed my cheeks lightly. "You are the most delicious being alive, always," she replied. "Your every emotion sates me." She leaned in and kissed me. Harder than she had been, and I melted into her.

The kiss turned slow and became a lingering motion of affection as I sat in her lap and simply enjoyed it. I said nothing else and did everything I could to avoid pulling from her, ignoring even my need to breathe.

Until Hale broke the kiss and lifted me up into her arms and off the bed. "I've something to show you," she told me.

My thoughts instantly went somewhere sensual. "Oh, really?" I asked and cocked a brow.

"Yes, Madriel has been helping me work on it whilst you rest," Hale said. This told me it most likely wasn't a fun, sexy time, but I wasn't going to count it out yet.

Hale carried me down the hallway with Fern trailing curiously behind us, and I realized we were headed to the library. "Oh, more books?" I asked with a smile. I had read through the books I borrowed from Madriel already, and a couple more they'd brought.

"You'll see," Hale insisted. "Close your eyes."

I did as I was told and leaned my head against her chest and shoulder, enjoying her arms around me.

I heard the door open in front of us and close behind us. The room was brighter than normal through my eyelids.

"Open now," Hale said.

I opened my eyes and adjusted to the light. Chandeliers above our heads had been polished and lit up. The room that had once been covered in dust and cobwebs was clean. The marble floor was warm and inviting, even with scratches and dents here and there. A large navy blue rug with swirling ornate silver details was spread out most of the length of the room.

"Oh, wow," I whispered. Hale set me down on my feet. I was steady.

The wooden shelves were still quite bare, but one was lined with several dozen paperbacks.

"I decided I could spare a few in the name of donation," Madriel spoke from behind us.

I jumped onto my toes and whirled around to look at them, my hand on my chest as I settled. "Oh, my god," I chuckled. "It looks amazing. There's even new chairs and a couch!" I said, looking to the side and motioning at the shiny leather furniture. "And the books! Thank you, Madriel." I wanted to run over and look at them immediately, but with my aching body, I knew that was probably not a good idea.

"It's nothing," they insisted whilst looking at their nails.

"It's everything," I corrected them, and looked to Hale. "It really...means a lot that you're making things more comfortable for me." I smiled at her, at them.

Hale smiled, baring sharp teeth and sending a shiver down my spine. "I've lived here too long for it to continue to be neglected," she said, "...you being here gives me more reason to fix it."

"Thank fuck for that," Madriel sighed. "I've been itching for a new project and helping get this place beautified and suitable for you, dear pet, is much welcome."

My ears heated at their words. I noticed Hale didn't seem bothered by the way they referred to me. They simply shifted closer to Madriel, and through the link we now shared, I could feel affection there as they looked at them.

Curiosity tickled me, but I wasn't sure how to voice it yet.

"Well. Since we're in here and I've been resting for days..." I said and moved to sit down on the couch. "I'd really enjoy having that book on the Midaworld read to me. Finally." I looked at them with a bit of impatience.

"You still haven't done that? Hale, I know reading isn't your forte, but the poor girl is wearing the mark of your teeth around her limbs." Madriel clicked their tongue and smirked.

Hale growled and walked over, grabbing the familiar book off the shelf and then sitting beside me. I placed myself gently into her lap and then looked up at Madriel.

"I suppose I should busy myself," they commented.

My brows furrowed. I felt sad at the idea of their absence. Whenever they came to visit the last few days, they were gone so quickly. "You can stay, if you'd like," I said.

Madriel paused where they stood before walking over to us and sinking down on the couch as well. They looked so much more elegant than I imagined either of us did. They brushed their long hair behind their shoulder and looked at Hale expectantly.

"Well, start reading."

Hale grumbled and handed me the book. "You hold it and turn the pages. It's safer for the pages," she explained. I couldn't help but smile. How strange it was that she could touch me with her claws and fingers, but was too nervous to turn the pages of a book.

"Alright," I replied and opened it up. I couldn't understand a single word, but I could guess the first few pages lined up with a well-organized list was the index.

I ran my fingers along the page before flipping until I reached the true start of the book. The cream-colored pages were oddly thin and fragile. Along the left side was a drawing of a tree with crooked and macabre branches that were devoid of any leaves or fruits. Peaking out from behind the tree were tiny clawed hands that scratched and dug into the bark.

"The first blood tree," Hale explained. I settled back into her chest, holding the book at just the right angle for her to read.

Her reading voice was rough and untrained, but as she settled into a rhythm, reading to me and Madriel about the history of the first blood tree and the very first demons to spill blood at its roots, I grew enamored.

I learned of the supposed first human to ever be taken to the Midaworld, and how they had begged for their life, but their blood and body were completely devoured. Of how the pain and suffering of their demonic lover had rippled out onto the land in a magic so powerful that it can still be felt in each thorn of the blood tree.

It was like a story from only my dreams, but it was the genuine history of the Midaworld. A realm that had existed just under my nose my entire life.

I noticed Madriel's slightly crinkled face as Hale read of the origin of the blood tree and thought of their lover they had lost. I was relieved for them as the subject seemed to change.

Demons of every kind called the Midaworld their home; but there was one group, The Elders, that were the oldest and most respected of them all.

"Do they enforce the rules?" I asked, mid sentence.

Hale looked down at me. "I am getting to that," she insisted.

I bit my lip and kept myself quiet. As she read, I spread out a bit more, and over time Madriel eased my legs into their lap and placed their hands over them.

The Elders used to enforce harsher and more strict rules, but over time, things relaxed, and with the Great War, many lives were lost and many rules were deemed more harmful than not. In the more recent years, The Elders became less of a ruling group and more of a historical face of the Midaworld. With very few true region wide regulations remaining, many areas sectioning themselves into districts and creating their own form of rule.

There was one regulation that they still oversaw. Claiming humans had become rare because of the danger it posed to the Midaworld. It was not illegal, so to speak, but if The Elders determined a human claimed might be of some danger to the Midaworlds secret, they may intervene.

My heart sunk into my stomach when I heard this. Hale's voice was low and slow as she read it. I knew now why she didn't want the others, aside from Madriel, to know that she had let me go and then I had come back to her.

Letting a human go after capturing them was strictly forbidden.

Hale's arm snaked around me and held me closer as anxiety crept up my spine.

I looked to Madriel as I felt their fingers gently caressing along my calve. Despite the coolness of their touch, the gesture was warm, and I realized, welcome and comforting.

18

SWEETEST TASTE

Hale

"How does aging work for humans here?" Renee asked. It felt rather random, given that I was in the middle of entangling her between my body and the couch in the library, our bodies pressed close together and lips playing.

She tilted her head to the side, her lips slightly swollen and red from our kisses.

I settled against her, careful not to put all of my weight on her.

"Days are shorter here and nights are longer," I explained, "years are longer, but you will age the same as you would in the human realm."

I watched her face fall and her gaze shift away from me. "I have limited time with you then," she says, "...though yes, I know, many decades."

I pressed my nose and cheek to her cheek and nuzzled there. "Drinking my blood can slow down your aging process," I told her, "...but it may also have other side effects if you partake consistently."

Her eyes lit up. "But I would live longer?" she asked.

I hummed out low and rumbling. "Yes," I said. I felt her fingers brush along the nape of my neck and into my hair. Her nails brushed my scalp, and a purr vibrated from my throat.

I wrapped my tail around one of her thighs and slid the end along the apex of her groin, caressing there casually. Renee's pulse sped up and her pupils widened.

"I drank your blood during the ritual, I know it helped me heal, but will it do anything else?" she inquired.

"Mm, no," I told her, "You drank enough to heal and be bound to me. That is all."

As I trailed fervent kisses up her cheek and across the bridge of her nose, she sighed. I feel the disappointment and anxiety emanating from her and sinking into me. I fed on it so diligently, hoping to ease her of it, but it remained.

"Your emotions are so very delicious," I croon. "But I am concerned. What are you thinking, Little One?"

Renee shifted underneath me and the soft form of her body squirming against mine drew a hot shiver up my spine. I ignored the urge to sink my hips between her thighs tight and grind.

"I want to be with you forever," she told me, "...but I'm worried forever won't exactly be..." she wiggled her head. "Well, you know, a very long time."

"Are you afraid I will not want to devour you as voraciously when you are older?" I asked.

Renee snorted. "No!" she insisted and shoved me slightly. She continued to push at my shoulders until I relented and leaned off her, sitting up.

"I just, I'm not sure how long your kind lives, but I know it's longer than a human," she said. "I want to have as much time with you as possible, not just humanly possible. So, I'm curious about this blood thing."

"I see," I hummed. "Are you curious about the effects besides age?"

She sat up and pulled her knees to her chest. "Of course," she narrowed her eyes. "I just can't imagine anything that would turn me off from living alongside you for decades more than normal."

"It's not incredibly common for demons to share their blood consistently, but when they have done so with humans...it results in a transformation of sorts," I explain. "You may hunger for blood, and your features may shift from their normal."

I felt the hesitation and curiosity in the air as Renee pondered this.

"So, along with slower aging, I might become more like a demon?" she asked.

"Yes," I replied. "It's not known for being pleasant."

She pursed her lips. "Hmm. I guess I'll be careful how often I partake then," she smirked.

"Are you saying you'd like to taste my blood again, Little One?" I leaned forward and loomed over her with my pulse drumming.

"I have to admit it...it tasted very interesting." She licked her lips absently. "I was overwhelmed when I tasted it, so I think I would need a second time for me to really determine how I feel about it." She nodded with a playful smile on her face.

"That can be arranged." I felt hot and itchy in my own skin. I had ever since the claiming ritual. Renee's healing was important, but every time that I pulled myself back from diving face first into her cunt, or licking a trail up her body, I felt another tight knot form in my core.

Renee giggled and put her foot up and on my chest, pushing me back and away from her. "Or I could tease you with my blood."

I grunted. "You do that every second you live," I replied.

Her face flushed that beautiful pink color, and I watched with hunger as it spread along her neck. I watched her pulse through the thin fragile skin of her throat. Such supple skin and tender flesh... My mouth watered and the fur at the back of my neck and shoulders bristled.

"Tell me about my blood. Does it taste like everything you could ever want?" Renee raised an eyebrow and smirked at me.

"And more," I told her. "Hot iron and sticky honey. That is what your blood tastes like."

Her face fell into a more relaxed and curious expression. "Iron I get. I've tasted my blood and...it tastes sort of like licking a rock to me, without the saltiness. But, honey?"

"Not human honey. The honey from this realm. They are two very different things," I explained. "Though they share similarities."

Renee snickered. *"Human honey."* She giggled another second and then bit her lip hard, making her face go straight. "What's the difference?"

"Honey here is sticky but thin, and the color of," I rolled over words in my head, "...orchids. Purple." I reached a hand out and brushed the back of my knuckles along one of her knees. Her temperature was so much cooler than my own, almost icy in comparison.

Renee's mouth formed a small o. "That's what that was on my food the other day," she said, "I was wondering but forgot to ask."

"The bread you have been indulging in is colored with it," I told her.

She hummed out happily. "I've really enjoyed tasting new foods. So familiar and yet...so alien."

Her genuine interest and delight leaked from every single pore, and I inhaled it so easily. It was so comfortable feeding from her emotions. I licked at them as they fanned out from all around her. I could not deny a specific interest in her pure raw anger and sadness the most, but there was a certain literal sugary sweetness to the aftertaste of her positive emotions that was addicting.

We sat in silence for a long moment, and I leaned back over her, wishing to kiss her once more. Just as I was pushing on her knees to move her legs down, she piped up with another question.

"How long were you with Valiri?" she asked.

I tensed briefly. "You have many questions today," I observed.

She rolled her eyes before they gazed back into mine. "You should get used to that."

I chuckled, the sound low in my chest, and pressed my lips to the side of her face once, then twice. "You make it so difficult to answer your questions when you look and smell so tempting, my mate," I husked.

Renee reached up and wrapped her arms around my neck. "You can continue lavishing me in kisses after you answer, promise," she said.

"Mm, I will hold you to that," I told her, and leaned back up and away. I settled into the couch, but only just. "Valiri and I were lovers off and on for many years. Many decades."

"It was never serious?" she inquired.

I looked at the ceiling lights, bored with the topic. "Perhaps it was once close to what you might consider serious. There was a period in which we lived together."

I felt and heard Renee shift into a more upright position.

"Why did it end?" Rippling waves of green and yellow came off her.

"You have no reason to be jealous," I told her, then answered. "Things were always fast and heavy with Valiri. We were obsessed with the carnal need one moment and bored the next, as there was little other connection."

"She didn't seem bored with you at the ritual," Renee commented.

I scoffed. "She is all but envy incarnate when it comes to what she doesn't possess, or in this case, who." I meet Renee's eyes and grab her hand. "I am yours, Little One. Let me soothe your concern by showing you just how much." I knew exactly what I wanted to do with Renee, and where I wanted to do it.

Renee squeezed my hand and pulled herself closer to me. I pulled her into my arms completely and lifted her from the couch. She gasped. I felt for her pain but felt shock instead, which soothed my own worries.

"Bed?" she suggested, her eyes lit up with excitement and desire.

"No, somewhere special." With that, I carried her out of the library. We remained in the house only long enough to secure something less revealing than her nightgown, much to my complete disinterest in covering her body, and she was still struggling to get it over her head as I was carrying her outside.

"Jeez, you're in a hurry hon'," Renee laughed as she finally wriggled the dress down her body while I held her securely in my arms with each squirm.

"That dress will not last long on you," I informed her with a low growl. I moved quickly through the trees to the left of my manor, knowing the way without truly thinking about it.

"Where are we going?" Renee asked from below.

"You'll see," I told her, and she was quiet. Trust rippled out from our bond.

It wasn't long until we were breaking from the trees and overlooking a wide section of cliffs. Several yards of tall blue and purple grass spread out before us. I set Renee down.

"Wow," Renee whispered. I watched as she stepped a couple feet forward, her wide eyes taking everything in. The early evening sky was glowing with the red sun beyond the gradients of the horizon. Both moons were already visible above us. Beyond the cliff, many staggering feet down, was a vast sea rocking with hungry charcoal waves. In the sky before us, slightly to the left, I could already see a glimmer.

"What is this?" Renee asked, motioning.

"That is the *Tingenim* Sea, *Temper* Sea, *Hungry* Sea," I explained.

Renee turned to me, her eyes lighting up. "I remember that, from the book." She beamed and looked back at it. "It's where...you can see a spot in which multiple realms connect." Her voice trailed off as she looked up and to the side, searching.

The longer I watched her, the more of her I wanted. Mind, body, soul, and I had her. I had tasted every single inch of her, and I wanted her still, again and again.

I stepped closer and took her hand, lifting it to the sky. "Right there," I positioned both of our hands. The glimmer in the sky was clearer, shifting and becoming more visible the longer I looked at it, and I hoped she could see it. "Do you see?" I asked.

I felt her excitement rise around me, sinking into me so deliciously, and the fire inside licked and gnawed at it. "I see!" she gasped.

In the sky there were several lines that blended into each other and the surrounding clouds, their jagged edges the stitches that connected multiple worlds. In this spot, we could gaze upon a small fraction of several realms at once.

"Wow," Renee said, voice awed, and she stepped back. Her back pressed against me and the breeze brought her scent to surround me fully.

I knelt down and pressed my lips to the crook of her neck. "I share this moment with only you," I whispered. My teeth ached in hunger and my burning heart throbbed with an affection I had never felt before.

Renee shivered against my touch and tilted her head to the side, offering me more of her neck. "You told me you'd show me you are mine," she hummed.

"And you promised much lavishing," I replied with a growl, my face still in her neck.

Renee turned around and wrapped her arms around my neck. I engulfed her in my arms as she sunk into me. Whose lips sought whose first was irrelevant. Kisses so deep and fervent. Her lips melted against mine so perfectly, so soft...so fucking good. I tangled her dress in my claws as I gripped her ass and hip with each hand. My tongue coaxed needy moans from her mouth as I danced around hers.

Thick need bled from us both and tangled until it was knotted and panting for release.

Unable to contain myself, I moved us both to the ground in the blink of an eye. Renee whimpered underneath me as I pressed her firmly to the grass. Her thighs spread for me without urging and I kissed down her chest, growling as I came to the damned fabric that covered it too damn much.

"I want to taste you, Little One," I told her. "I need you. I feel as though I might peel out of my skin if I don't devour every bit of your needy, slutty little desire." The world was growing dim to me, only she existed.

Renee shivered, and her hands slid to my shoulders. Even in my heady fog, I could sense her discomfort. She was still sore.

"I'm not sure you can handle what I want to give you," I growled.

She gripped me tighter and arched into me. "No! No, I can. Please, I want you too...I need you."

I could smell her wet pussy from where I was, and the scent sent a shiver of my down my spine. My hips rocked against her at their own will and my tail wrapped around her thighs, snaking between them and me.

I groaned and forced myself to lean up and away from her despite the wanton desire burning me from the inside out.

"Nooo," Renee whined and tried to reach for me, but her arms couldn't quite reach.

I huffed out a puff of hot air as I rolled to sit on my ass in the grass and stared at her hungrily.

"Soon," I told her. "Soon I will ravage you to our heart's content."

Renee propped herself up on her elbow and looked at me while biting her lip. She kept her thighs spread, with her dress draped between them. A bit of moisture dampened the fabric, and I eyed it like the last supper.

"What if I help myself and you watch?" Renee asked. "You will be able to feed off of that, right?"

The edges of my body ignited. "I will," I confirmed. My eyes meet hers heatedly. "Go on, show me how wet you are, my mate."

I watched as Renee hurriedly reached down and pulled her dress up from between her thighs to expose herself. That triangle of dark curls that framed her pussy came into view and I watched with bated breath as she parted her lips with her fingers and showed her hard clit and aching hole.

I licked my lips, feeling my cunt throb in the confines of my clothing.

"So wet. Give yourself the attention you need," I ordered.

Renee obeyed me without hesitation and rubbed her clit in slow circles. Soft moans escaped her throat, and she wobbled slightly, struggling to keep herself upright on one arm.

I knew if I came any closer to her, even to sit behind her and steady her, I wouldn't be able to resist her. So I stayed where I was, my eyes glued to her, and my claws sinking into the dirt underneath them.

"Hale," she moaned. She rocked her hips against her hand and fell to lie flat in the grass as she touched herself.

My breath quickened as I watched her tug the dress up and until it was over her head and toss it to the side, her small night gown with it.

"Oh, Little One, you tempt me," I growled under my breath.

Renee's free hand slid up to her chest and caressed one of her breasts, her fingers pinching softly at her nipple. I felt my own nipples tingle as I felt her pleasure and arousal shiver off of her body and into mine.

"That's it," I praised her, "such a Good Girl, keep going. I can taste it." The air around me was thick and needy. On my tongue, the flavor of sex and passion was overwhelming even without touching her. I fed on those needy emotions greedily as Renee continued to work herself up.

Her pussy glistened with slick, and her hips quivered. I felt my own hips twitch underneath me. My vision was red hot and focused entirely on her.

"Fill yourself with your fingers," I told her.

The ground pulled up underneath my hands, roots tearing.

Renee slid two of her fingers into her pussy with ease and arched her back as she fucked herself with them quickly.

"Oh, fuck!" She gasped and panted for breath.

I could feel my breathlessness growing, and my skin was covered in goosebumps, every inch, even that which was under my fur.

"Yes," I growled. "Look at you, filling that pretty little pussy, gah." Pleasure rippled along my arms and down into my groin. "F-Fuck, pet, faster. Let me hear you!"

Renee whimpered as she added another finger and fucked herself faster, her fingers curling more. "Yes, oh...Mistress, please! Tell me-Tell..." she struggled to get the words out, but I knew what she needed. I watched her with my drooling mouth and soaked cunt, eyes darting up to her greedy little hand that massaged and flicked her nipples down to her hole that she finger fucked so delightfully. I could even see her other hole clench in pleasure.

"Come for me, mmn," I begged. My core was a tight ball of energy that was desperate for release. I lifted a hand and groped my breast through my leather top, feeling my nipple harden underneath my touch.

I soaked in every single glittering shade of Renee's pleasure and affection as it radiated off her in tantalizing waves. Devouring her every moan and hitched breath as she grew closer to her own undoing.

Renee's moans grew louder and more desperate until finally her hips lifted ever so slightly above the ground and she shivered hard. Her come squirted a short distance onto the blades of grass between her thighs, and the rest dripped out of her slowly.

At this same moment, I felt an orgasm of my own quiver in my thighs, despite having not touched my pussy at all. It was a phantom feeling that shot across my groin and clenched inside of me. I tossed my head back and moaned.

As the pleasure fizzled out, I was buzzing from head to toe.

I looked at Renee and saw that she was lying there limp with her wet hand on her stomach. Her eyes were half lidded as they focused on the sky and her mouth was agape.

Feeling satisfied with my meal, I could comfortably move toward her and lay beside her. I traced her jawline with my claw and turned her face to me.

"Good Girl," I whispered. "Pretty girl."

Renee smiled softly, her expression blissfully senseless. "Pretty monster."

My iron heart squeezed, and I leaned to kiss her bare shoulder up and until I reached the crook of her neck.

"I *love* you," Renee whispered.

I stilled for just a moment before looking up to meet her gaze. There were three worlds connecting in the sky above us, but there were thousands in those eyes.

"I love *you*," I replied. The words were almost foreign on my tongue. When was the last time I had spoken them? They felt right.

I draped my arm over her bare breasts and we laid there until the sun had completely set and the dark of the night surrounded us. It wasn't until Renee's stomach growled that I realized I should feed her again.

"Have I left you famished?" I asked quietly.

She laughed and nuzzled into my shoulder. "Mm, just a bit. You know...I'm actually kind of craving that cake you fed me once."

I melted into her affections. "Ah, yes?" I replied, remembering the way I had fed it to her.

"Yes. It was strange at first, but I think the tastes here are really growing on me," she admitted.

"I would hope so," I nipped at her face as she tilted it up. My head was dizzy with pleasure and all I could think about was making her happy in any way possible.

"Could we get some?" she asked, her pupils still blown wide with desire.

A purr vibrated in my chest as I thought. "I will get it," I told her. "Anything you want, I will bring you." I pulled away from her and sat up.

"Just the dessert," she smiled and sat up as well.

"You stay there, relax," I told her, "no one will bother you here."

She eyed me curiously. "Are you sure?" Her voice was small and tired.

"I will be gone only a moment," I replied. The world was small and meaningless compared to the little piece of delight that we had there on the grassy cliff side under the moons. Every inkling of common sense had left my head, for better or worse. I simply wanted to find the cake and feed it to her under the stars.

As I stood up, Renee tugged her clothing back on, but stayed on the ground. Before I knew it, I was rushing through the forest even faster than I went while carrying her. I had no trouble finding what I was looking for. A shop open all hours of the night was not at all surprised to see me there, nor did they question my single purchase.

Renee would have been able to count the minutes I was gone on one hand, and it was in time less than those five fingers that I was making my way back to her with her beautiful face in my mind's eye.

As I made my way through the trees, I felt a sudden tug at our bond. It was desperate and alarmed. Confusion waved across me, and I stopped in my tracks as a rubber banding effect snapped within me. The pain made me physically recoil, and I grunted. Despite this, I moved forward quicker now. As I broke the tree line, I felt numbness settle into my neck and down into my chest.

"Little One?" I said, holding the box of food in my hands.

I looked upon the empty imprint in the grass where I had left her sitting. It took a fraction of a second for me to process, but it felt like a lifetime all the same.

Renee was gone.

19

VENOM

Renee

One moment I was lying in the grass staring up at two luminous moons, wondering who else was doing the same, and the next...I was taking two arachnid fangs to the neck. The first thing that hit me was the stabbing pain. It plunged much deeper than Hale's teeth, violating my very flesh to the deepest points. The next was a numbness that settled over my entire body, starting from my throat to my toes. My vision grew blurry, but before I was completely unable to see, I saw her. Valiri.

Her dark gray and black splotched skin and that fuzzy short hair that covered her from cheek bones to cleavage, her many arms included. Fear flooded my psyche, and I tried to scream Hale's name, but my voice wouldn't come. It was like one of those nightmares where I tried desperately to get anyone's attention, but my mouth was simply left agape and lungs breathless.

As I faded out of consciousness, I could feel a wave of anxiety that wasn't my own hit me. Hale already knew something was wrong. She'd help me, she'd save me, I knew she would.

All I could smell was petrichor—the damp mossy scent of dirt after rain—and blood. My vision was still blurry, but I realized I could move my body again. Well, at least I could wiggle my fingers and toes. With the sensation of movement came an ache accompanied by a tingling not similar to whacking your elbow on a hard surface. Except it didn't seem to go away as I flexed my fingers and toes.

I groaned and squeezed my eyes shut tighter, wishing that I could simply wake up and be safe and sound in Hale's arms. No spider ex-girlfriends to be had.

"Ah, you're awake. I underestimated the effects my venom would have on you," Valiri said from above me. "For a moment there, I thought you were dead. I'll have to be careful, you're much weaker than I expected." She mused.

My vision started to clear, and her unnerving features towered over me. Her arms reached for me and I could do nothing but voice my displeasure in the indistinct sounds from my throat.

I looked around and realized we were in a cave. That explained the smell.

"I really thought you'd die during claiming," she said. A disappointed frown painted her face as her many eyes darted about mine. "Then of course you didn't, so I really expected you'd be harder to put down." She clicked with her lips and teeth.

I sucked in a breath that brought pain to my ribs. "Fuck you." I hadn't really intended on saying that, it was just the first thing that rolled off my tingling lips. My mouth felt a bit like I'd just had a cavity filled.

"Oh, don't pretend you wouldn't like that," Valiri wrapped

several of her arms around me and pulled me up with effortless strength until I was suspended a foot or so above the hard cave floor. "I saw you making a mess of yourself for my Hale, like a dirty bitch in heat, aren't you?" She was grinning at me, but her eyes were cold with envy.

More feeling was returning to my body in painful twitches. I could squirm ever so slightly against her tight hold. My jealousy was a warm wave that traveled up my stomach and squeezed at my heart. Or perhaps that was bile...

"She's mine," I spat. "I'm her *mate*. Not you." Pain washed over the tight bundles of nerves in my body as I regained more and more feeling. Closing my hands into fists felt impossible, the muscles rigid.

"Mine!" Valiri shrieked in my face. Droplets of burning saliva spotted my cheeks and nose.

Something sharp slashed at my back and cut through my skin just as easy as the fabric. I screamed through gritted teeth and screwed my eyes shut. It happened again, icy cold and piercing, and I realized it was her claws.

Fear and anger ran through me as writhed against the pain, and even then...arousal build up in my stomach. It wasn't the same as with Hale. I didn't feel invigorated by it. Instead, I felt dread.

"Little human bitch," Valiri snarled. "How Halelyn hasn't consumed you whole, I don't know. I thought them smarter than this. Keeping you around...as a pet."

Halelyn? The name swarmed my head for a moment, but then another wracking pain hit me and I saw red.

"Let me go!" I hissed. "She's gonna kill you!"

Fuck, it felt like my bones were on fire and trying to dig their way out of my body to find relief. Every inch of my skin prickled and throbbed on top of them.

"Oh, she's gonna kill you good," I panted. If I'd ever had any sense for not making the situation worse, I lost every once of that now.

Suddenly I was flipped upside down and all the blood ran to my head. Sticky webbing weaved around my legs as Valiri made her way around me with ease and suspended me upside down in her web, but left the top half of my body uncovered and dangling. My tattered and torn dress slipped off over my head and my nightgown just barely hung on.

I felt Valiri's claws drag along my stomach, but this time they burned me instead of slicing at my skin. She must have coated them with her venom. I gritted my teeth and tried not to make any sounds. I didn't want her to get any satisfaction from the pain she was causing me. My head was throbbing as blood pooled in it, and paired with the tight webs around my legs, my feet grew cold.

"She might call you her mate, but all you are is a pet, you know that, don't you?" Valiri asked me, but there was no pause for me to answer. "Just her play thing until she gets too hungry to resist."

I gasped as she dug into my back with one of her claws in a slow, agonizing circle. Blood dripped down my body and onto the cave floor. I could hardly see again.

"She loves me!" I huffed.

Valiri laughed. "Oh, you poor thing, so diluted. Really, I'm doing both of you a favor by ending you before she does," she put on a mock caring voice.

My vision was all black specks and flickering lights.

Drip. Drip.

I wanted Hale's suffocatingly warm arms around me. I wanted to bury my face in the crook of her neck and shoulder and stay safe and sound there for all of eternity. My heart ached with each cruel thing Valiri said, but I didn't believe her. I couldn't. Not when I felt and saw the utter devotion in Hale as she claimed me, and as she held me and fed me for days afterward.

The demon before me was bitter and jealous. I knew this, but it didn't make the pain she caused me any less excruciating.

"W-What do you get out of this?" I asked. My voice felt distant. "She won't forgive you."

"How sweet, you think she'll remember you long enough to hold a grudge," Valiri gripped my face with one of her hands and her claws pierced halfway into my cheeks. My head filled with static. "We're demons, we hunt you, sometimes we fuck you, and when you die, we do it again."

My eyes burned with hot tears that had nowhere to go but back into my stinging eyes. My breath hitched as I struggled to keep myself from crying.

"That's it, cry and whine, it's so delicious," Valiri's tongue swept across my eyelids and I shuttered.

"Hale," I cried out. All I could think about was those three words we had spoken to each other only moments before I was taken.

I love you.

"Don't you worry about her," she said, "soon you'll be in the ground and *I* will be the one she fucks for comfort, again and again."

"You don't know her." I tried to squirm, but I could hardly move yet again.

"I've known her a hundred years, and you think you know her better?" Valiri cackled, "You are truly a pathetic specimen. I know everything she likes, and I can handle it better than you ever will."

Valiri struck me harder and deeper than before. I screamed, unable to hold it in, my body quivering. "Because you're a pitiful, fragile thing who will learn her place in death."

Searing pain took over every one of my senses.

Hale, please help me.

20

THE ONE WITH RAGE

Hale

I all but dissolved the front door of Madriel's home into splinters and dust as I came barreling through. Normally I might have made my way home and used the portal between our land, but I was much to wound up to even begin to think of that.

The moment I'd discovered Renee was no longer where I had foolishly left her, I knew that I had fucked up. My post-sex fogged brain had been certain that she would be safe there on the distant plot of my land surrounded by trees and starlight. I was only gone a few minutes and yet something had happened. I felt her pain and fear for only a moment until suddenly it was gone and replaced by a black nothingness.

I had never been truly scared in my entire life, even death was something I was fully willing to face one day if I had to, but...as I became aware of just how empty our emotional bond felt, I feared the worst.

"Madriel!" I called. My hands were balled into fists. I whisked around the corridor searching, I knew they were there. They had to be. I couldn't waste much time looking for them to help me when I needed to be looking for her.

At the last second, when I was ready to leave and go about

my hectic search alone, Madriel came rushing over with a golden hairbrush in hand.

"Hale, what's going on?" Madriel asked. "You look absolutely rattled, and that's a new one for you."

"It's Renee, I took her to the cliffs to see the sky, and..." I trailed off, uncertain of telling Madriel the full truth. Before I could get anything else out, however, they seemed to catch on.

"Renee? What's happened to her?" they asked, "*who* happened to her more specifically?"

"It's Valiri, I know it is, it has to be. She's taken her." I growled and blue fire licked at my palms.

Madriel set the brush down on a nearby table. I expected them to tell me they told me so, perhaps gaze at me with cool condemnation, I deserved it. Instead, their eyes were equally panicked as I felt.

"I wouldn't hold it against her. How did she get to her, did you leave Renee alone?" Madriel asked, and then shook their head. "Forget it, that's not important right now. We have to find her."

At that moment, I feel a ripple in my connection to Renee. It's faint, but I feel her confusion. "When she was taken I could not feel her, but I'm starting to again." I explained.

"Valiri must have knocked her out," Madriel says. "You can use your connection to find her. You just have to focus. Let's go."

I said nothing else as I moved beside Madriel outside. "She wouldn't take Renee to her home," I insisted. I cursed under my breath and closed my eyes to try and focus as the breeze ruffled my fur.

Pain flicked up my arms, but I couldn't pinpoint anything else.

"Damn it," I huffed. "Fucking Valiri, she's hurting Renee. I know it."

I opened my eyes and looked at Madriel, who was more tense than I had seen them in a long time.

"Why is she doing this? To spite me?" I growled and waved a scorching hand at the grass, watching it ignite for a split second and fizzle out into smoke.

"Renee is in the way of her crawling back into your bed," Madriel hissed.

"...she won't hesitate to kill Renee," I glared into the night.

Madriel put a hand on my arm. "Focus, and we'll find her before she's tired of tutoring her."

I took a deep breath and stepped forward, letting the hazy bond between Renee and I flood through me and guide me. The feeling of being led, every step, was uncertain. Was I moving right because I truly felt her, or was I simply guessing?

My breath hitched as our bond grew stronger again, and I felt a stinging pain cross into my mental barrier. It did not hurt me, but I could feel how hurt she was.

"I can feel her stronger," I huffed. "This way." I moved quicker, certain now.

Madriel followed behind me without hesitation. Their wings spawned from behind them lightning fast, large, the same gray color as their skin.

I groaned and leaned toward the ground as more pain struck Renee. Again and again. I could all but taste her blood in my mouth, and I knew somehow this meant she was losing it.

We were miles from where Renee had been taken already.

"I'm going to rip her fucking throat out!" I growled. I dug my claws into the ground and ripped the earth up as I stood. I panted and my shoulders lifted with each breath.

"We have to find her for you to do that!" Madriel hissed at me. They were growing more frantic as the moments passed sickeningly slow.

I moved as fast as I could through tall grass and bulbous trees that grew thicker and mustier the deeper we entered the forest. The ground grew harder and bare under foot as we traveled.

Each lash of pain I felt threw Renee and I's bond sent me reeling forward with more and more intensity. She was close; I knew it.

We came to an opening in the trees and I stepped out, raking the scene before me with my burning eyes. On the breeze, the scent of iron and honey tickled my senses.

"Blood." I gnashed my teeth. "I can smell her blood."

"Me too," Madriel whispered. "That means she's lost a lot of it."

Before us lay a beach front of coarse wet sand and rocks. Within the hilly landscape were several natural caves.

Despite the pain it caused me, I dug deeper within myself to grasp the connection and beg for guidance. The scent of her blood aided me, but it also drove me wild.

"This way," I huffed out. The beach was soon behind me as I made my way to a cave further back than the others.

Hale, please help me.

Renee's voice was a desperate cry in my head that cracked the stone of my heart. All hunger, all desire, had been washed from me in that moment. All I could think about was wringing Valiri's neck until she was limp and cold, and getting my mate out of there.

The cave's entrance was dark, but I could see perfectly.

"Are you sure?" Madriel asked.

I twitched as the scent of blood grew stronger. So much blood.

"Yes," I growled. The sound echoed gently. A whimper from deeper prompted me forward in an instant. Light emanated from the back of the damp cave and the first thing my eyes landed on was Renee. She was strung up in thick sticky webbing, hung upside down and dripping with blood. I could feel how tired she was, how much she wished to give into the fading fuzziness. It danced across me and brought more panic to my chest.

"Valiri!" I roared. I snapped my head over to see her leaning against a cave wall, her arms folded.

"It's only for the best," she replied coolly. "You know how delicious she is, she wouldn't have lasted very long, lover, and you know it."

My hands balled into fists so tight that my claws cut into my palms.

"What have you done?" The words came from gritted teeth.

She opened her mouth to speak, but I was already launching myself at her quick and hard.

Her many arms gave her an advantage, but my strength gave me mine. My claws slashed at her face and torso wildly, even as she swiped at me.

"This is a mistake!" Valiri shrieked. "You will have no one without me!"

I screamed in her face, seeing only red, as I picked her up by her waist and slammed her down onto the hard rock floor. I pinned her beneath one of my knees and grabbed her head.

She must've sliced me a few times, there was blood dripping from my neck and face, but I could feel nothing.

"No...I won't...leave Hale here," Renee's voice cracked quietly.

I turned my head to see Madriel having pulled Renee down from the bed and pried her from its clutches; they were holding her in their arms but she tried to struggle against them.

"Go!" I demanded. "Get her out. Now!"

This distraction was just enough for Valiri to sink her fangs into my arm, not once, but twice, and ice filled my veins. My arms burned, but I slammed my fist into her chest as I toppled over beside her. Fire lit up in my hands.

I watched Madriel place Renee to the ground in one quick movement and rush over.

Just as Valiri was about to inject me with her venom again, Madriel pounced on top of her.

"No you don't, bitch!" They hissed at her, fangs bared.

With Valiri flailing her head and arms wildly, trying to get Madriel off of her, pulling at their hair and clothing, there was an in.

I smashed my hand into Valiri's face, blue fire and all, and held it there as she screamed in agony, her eyes and face burning and melting to a crisp. I pushed Madriel off of her and straddled her body myself, placing my other burning hand onto her chest.

Valiri grew weak and her body twitched underneath me.

"Please..." she whispered from her disfigured mouth. The scent of burning necrotic flesh heavy in the air.

"This was your choice," I choked out, and plunged my burning hand into her chest, through her sternum and rubs until her heart was in my hand. Blood spurted and oozed as I ripped it out of her chest. The sound of ripping and cracking accompanied the viscera.

Valiri's last breath was a tormented gasp, and then she was completely still.

My breath remained heavy, and all I could see was her corpse and blood. Anger and pain surrounded me so fully that I could not escape it even then that the threat was gone.

Her heart dropped from my fist, flopping to the ground and rolling once away from her body. I stared at my bloodied hand.

"Hale," Madriel spoke slowly. "It's done. She's dead. We've got Renee."

My eyes darted over and I saw Renee there, leaning against Madriel, just barely standing. She was naked and her peachy skin was littered with coagulating lacerations that made my mouth water and my stomach clench.

A low growl slipped through my teeth as I looked at her. Her eyes were barely open. She looked...so fragile. My muscles twitched.

"Hale," she whispered. Her voice was so sweet. The sound flipped a switch in my head, and I felt the rush start to fade away.

I stood up from the sound, and my muscles relaxed.

Madriel exhaled with relief. "We need to get her home," they said.

I was at Renee's side in an instant and took her into my arm. She closed her eyes and nuzzled up against me. With that, Madriel and I were making the journey to my home, where we could fully evaluate her injuries.

21

CERTAINTY

Renee

Hale's arms were wrapped around me, safe and secure. A gentle breeze passed us and brought the salty scent of the ocean to my nose. We were overlooking the horizon as the sun was rising, but it wasn't the sky of the Midaworld. I squinted as I realized this. We were most certainly in the human realm. I looked around us and saw other people relaxing on towels in the sand. Children were running and playing in the water, splashing each other and tossing a beach ball every which way. Yet they didn't react to Hale's monstrous form.

I turned to look up at Hale and saw her gazing back down at me. Her feline eyes were glistening with tears.

"Why are you crying?" I asked. I had never seen her cry before. It made my heart ache. I reached a hand up and brushed my fingers just under her eye on her cheek. Hot tears rolled down my knuckles to my wrist.

Everything around us felt fuzzy and distant all of the sudden.

Hale didn't reply to me. As I opened my mouth to speak, nothing would come out.

I took a breath, and at this same moment, reality came rushing back to me.

My eyes opened as I gasped for air and sat up. Pain stung at my flesh as I did so, and I groaned.

"Careful," Hale insisted, and I was pushed gently onto my back again.

As my vision cleared, I saw her sitting beside me. I was lying on my bed, our bed, in the dimly lit bedroom and something warm and wet was touching my left thigh.

I moaned tiredly and looked down. Madriel was there, dabbing at my skin with a washcloth. My face flushed, but I was in no position to object.

"Oh, Renee," Hale whispered and leaned down, nuzzling her face against my forehead. "I was so worried."

What happened with Valiri came to me in flickers. I could remember the tight webbing around my legs and hips, and the piercing of her fangs and numbness of the venom.

I wiggled my fingers. They didn't feel quite right. A zing of pain shot up my forearm into my elbow.

"Many of the cuts are more shallow than I thought," Hale said as she leaned back to look at me. "...You could drink my blood to heal. You should heal faster this second time."

I blinked at her. "Are you sure?" I asked.

"Yes. I cannot bear to see you with Valiri's marks," Hale replied. Her face contorted painfully.

I looked at my arms and down my bare chest to my stomach. I looked a bit like I'd gotten into a fight with a giant piece of paper. I couldn't help but giggle.

Madriel looked up at me with a nervous look. I realized Hale looked concerned, too.

"I'm feeling...a bit loopy," I replied.

Hale brushed the pads of her fingers along my cheek. "I must mend you," she said.

I watched with fixed eyes as she bit into her own wrist. She held it to me, and I found that my mouth, strangely, watered. I latched onto her wrist and the dripping coal black blood, lapping it up with my tongue and swallowing.

Hale's other hand moved to the back of my head.

"Good Girl," she purred.

Madriel had stopped cleaning me now.

My eyes were closed and the only thing on my mind was how hot Hale's blood was. The taste was almost like ash, floral ash, but something about it urged me to swallow it in heady slurps.

Hale grunted softly as my hands latched onto her arm tightly.

"Hm. Greedy little thing," Madriel's voice was a curious mumble nearby. I felt warmth in my core but ignored it.

I finally had to come up for air, panting and licking my lips, and blood dripped down my chin. A heavy shiver ran up my spine.

Hale pulled her wrist from me. I eyed her face and neck. I remembered, vaguely, Valiri swiping at her, but all I could see were thin lines of mostly healed wounds on her body. Her wrist was already almost healed.

"How are you feeling?" Hale asked.

I sighed. "Stronger already," I told her. "My fingers still feel weird, though." I flexed them again. I felt oddly calm despite what happened with Valiri.

"That should pass," Madriel said. I looked over to see them shifted their weight off the bed.

In spite of Hale's order to stay lying down, I slowly sat up and reached for Madriel.

"Come here," I insisted. They looked at me, confused, but shuffled closer on the bed.

I leaned closer and pressed my lips to their cheek. It was cold, but soft. I lingered for only a second. "Thank you for helping," I told them.

As I leaned a back into bed, Madriel touched their cheek and looked at me with conflicted eyes. "O-Of course," they muttered. They opened their mouth to say something else, but slid off the bed. Just as they were about to step forward, they spoke. "His name was Luca. My mate."

My brow furrowed. "Thank you for telling me."

Madriel simply nodded, eyes going glassy, and turned away.

"I'll leave you too alone. Let me know how she's doing later."

Part of me wanted to ask Madriel to stay, but I got the feeling they would have if they wanted to. I looked to Hale, who couldn't seem to keep her eyes off me.

My brow furrowed. "It's not your fault, you know," I said.

She slid into the bed beside me and pulled the thick comforter over us. The heat of her body made the space under the blanket toasty and cozy.

"It is," she replied. "...but it won't happen again. My Little One." She slid a gentle arm underneath me and pulled me into her chest.

I cuddled into her silently for a long while, but tears began to form in my eyes. That emotional numbness wearing off.

"Valiri said things to me..." I said. My voice was a quiet sound, almost muffled against her skin and fur. "Would it be dramatic of me to say her words almost hurt more than the lashing?"

A low growl rumbled in Hale's chest against my face, and it was relaxing. "She was good at cutting deep with her words."

I snuggled tighter into her, ignoring the aching and tingling across my body, just wanting to be closer.

"Do you want to tell me what she said?" Hale asked. Her hands pressed into my back, large and steady.

My eyes were closed, brow furrowed. I could see blood and the dark cave walls behind my eyelids, but there was nothing in particular that caused my sense of shakiness.

"Just lies," I replied. "She doubted us being mates and said I'm just your plaything."

Hale's arms tightened comfortably for just a second. "Lies indeed," she said.

"Not that I...can't be your plaything sometimes," I mumbled, a small smile on my face. "I like it, in the right situation." Thinking about being close with her helped ease my discomfort.

"I like you in all forms, my mate," Hale told me and her lips pressed to my cheek, then my temple and hair.

Fern climbed up over the blanket and settled down on it in the groove where both of our bodies met. Hale's arm shifted to include her underneath it, and I peaked a hand out of the blanket to touch Fern's paw.

My body and mind was tired, but I found myself nervous about sleeping. A small part of me was worried that I would wake up and be back in Valiri's clutches.

"Valiri is dead?" I asked, needing confirmation. "Right?"

I could feel Hale's breath against my bare shoulder. "She is dead."

Her voice was low.

"You're positive?" I chewed at my lip.

Fern wiggled more firmly into both of us and then loafed with her face flat against the blanket.

"I am very certain," Hale murmured. "You don't remember?"

I frowned. "Not really. Everything was hazy when you showed up." I sighed and tried to relax more. I flinched as I drifted off and yanked myself back into being awake.

"Are you alright?" Hale asked, her husky voice laced with concern.

I squirmed slightly, causing Fern to shift and look up at us for a second with, I swear, an annoyed express, and then face plant again.

"I'll be okay," I replied.

It was quiet for a moment longer.

"I can't promise no one else will pose a threat again in the future," Hale told me. "...but I will protect you with my life."

My stomach knotted up. "I trust you," I insisted. "I want to be here, no matter what."

I tilted my head up to look into her face and Hale leaned down and kissed me. I placed a hand on her jawline as I kissed her back, slow and soft. Her teeth nipped my lips slightly, and it made me flush.

"I should feed you, get you water," Hale said as she broke the kiss.

I shook my head. "No, I don't want you to leave." The words came out sounding more frantic than I intended.

Hale just eyed my face and then tucked hers into my shoulder once more.

We stayed like this for a while, and I fought sleep for as long as I could.

The last thing I heard before I finally drifted off was Hale's raspy voice.

"You're safe, Little One."

EPILOGUE - THREE WEEKS LATER

Renee

"Are stretches Madriel taught you helping?" Hale asked as she set some food down on the coffee table in the library.

I was sitting in a comfortable chair with one of my arms bent straight and the other easing my hand back toward my wrist. My brow was furrowed.

"A little bit," I replied. "They're not very comfortable to do, but they've been giving me a couple of hours of relief."

Hale sat down across from me. I wished she was sitting with me, but I knew I needed to eat rather than get distracted by her affections.

I sighed as I finished stretching. The tingling in my hands and arms had not gone away yet, and if I tried to write by hand, my hands would cramp up within minutes. I could normally write without pain for an hour, at least if not more.

I looked up into Hale's eyes and saw guilt there. I knew she still blamed herself for what happened, but I didn't. We had both been so out of it...

"I'm definitely feeling better than last week, though," I told her. I leaned towards the table and pulled the bowl of food into my lap. It was warm against my thighs and felt nice.

"The food is helping. It's comforting, and delicious," I smiled. "Plus, I'm pretty proud of the bread I made." I looked at the purple slices tucked next to the food.

Hale's lips turned up slightly. "You have certainly adjusted remarkably, my pet."

I ate diligently, enjoying how Hale watched me as if it was the most entertaining show she had ever seen. Her glowing red eyes were full of affection.

"Are you going to read to me today?" I asked between bites. "We only have one chapter left of *'Midnight Ruin'.*" I licked the salty, peppery goodness from my lips.

Hale cocked her head. "Perhaps later," she replied. "I have a different idea for the beginning of this evening."

Butterflies fluttered in my stomach and heated my thighs. Even with the lingering chronic pain I was dealing with, I still couldn't get enough of Hale.

"Oh, do you now?" I asked playfully and licked my spoon slower than needed.

She hummed, the sound a low vibration in the air. I could feel her desire for me palpable in the air. The feeling twisted and interlocked with the accompanying concern and affection.

"Maybe I should come over there right now," I wiggled gently. I felt the slight tenseness of my back muscles, but it didn't hurt like my arms and hands did.

Hale's gaze burned hotter. "Finish eating."

I smirked. "Yes, Mistress." I took another bite, starting in on the bread to get the rest of my food scooped up. Hale had learned how to better portion food so that I wasn't so stuffed when I finished eating, but pleasantly full and sated.

I set the bowl on the table and put my hands in my lap. My knees bounced anxiously.

"What is this plan for tonight?" I asked her.

Hale stood up and I let my eyes graze her tall, broad body from her clawed feet to the swell of her chest and her eyes. Her black hair was pulled back in a long single braid that Madriel had done for her the night before when they'd been over.

"Heat has been helping your pain," Hale said.

I nodded slowly, wondering where she was going with this.

"...and you have practically been squirming with desire for something that ignites your passion like being chased does."

Blush rose from my neck to my cheeks, but I nodded enthusiastically. "I hate not being able to run as much right now," I frowned. "...but I want you in every way, Hale, I'll take whatever I can get."

Hale smirked, crooked and prideful. "I'll give you everything I have, always," she stepped closer and leaned down to me. Her claws ran gently up my neck to my jaw, where she gripped it and leaned down to kiss me. I kissed her back, slow and deepening. I could get lost in her lips for a lifetime, and I was certain I would.

"You didn't really answer my question," I said at the same moment I realized it. My words were spoken against her lips.

Hale's forked tongue peaked out to lip her lips before she pulled back.

"I was getting to it. You distracted me, my minx." She took a step back, as if to distance herself for good measure. "Playing with fire may ease some of your pain and turn you on all the same," she said. I watched as her palms lit up with a soft glow that flickered out to her fingertips were orange and yellow fire licked at the flesh but did not burn.

An image of her hands but with blue violent flames slammed into Valiri's face flooded my mine. My breath hitched in my throat and I brushed it away. These flames were different, I could see. Blue blames were the hottest they could get, these orange and yellow flames mimicked that of a campfire, warm and crackling.

I realized I was staring and shifted my gaze to her face. "I'm interested." I had wanted to say something sexier, but it was all I could get out of my mouth. My suddenly parched mouth.

"Do you remember our safe word from the ritual?" Hale asked. My pussy throbbed at the thought, surprising me and causing me to squish my thighs together.

"Yes," I told her, "Ruby."

I had chosen the word because it was the dazzling color of her eyes when she gazed at me after we kissed or fucked. Not quite the burning blood red they were beforehand.

With that, Hale extended a hand to me. I took her hand with no hesitation.

"How rough can you handle, Little One?" she asked me as she towered above.

I chewed at my lip before I answered, trying to honestly mull it over. "Moderately, but be more careful with my arms, and no ropes, please."

"As you wish."

With that, Hale lead me to the fireplace, still in the library. It was flickering with a low warmth. I'd adjusted to the temperature difference in the Midaworld, and since I'd been chocked full of venom weeks prior, I'd actually been more cold than usual.

"On your knees," Hale ordered. Her tone and words showing me the shift in situation. We were no longer casually talking.

I did as she asked of me and sunk to my knees on the rug in front of the fireplace. It was soft and plush. I tilted my head up to look at her. She was so powerful and magnificent that the feeling radiated to me and made me feel even more confident.

"You are worshiping at an altar," Hale crooned. "Yet you're so over dressed. I'll have to fix that." She knelt down and her hands found the hem of my dress. She pulled it over my head, revealing my naked and scarred body. Only three distinct scars remained. She tossed my dress to the side and ran her fingers along my neck where her sharp teeth had left an impact on my flesh that would remain with me forever.

Hale brushed my hair behind my shoulders and gathered the curls up just tight enough to wrap a strip of leather that was secured around her wrist around them. It kept my hair out of face and gave her more access to my neck and shoulders.

As I sat bare before her, Hale's eyes wandered me without shame.

I swore I could smell her wet arousal through her leather shorts and couldn't help but open my mouth and stick my tongue halfway out as I looked up at her. Showing her what I wanted.

Hale purred. "Not yet, sweet," she told me. "Fire first, fucking later."

I stuck my tongue back into my mouth, but kept my eyes up and on her. I watched as fire came to her fingertips again.

"Close your eyes."

I hesitated only for a second, as I had wanted to see more, but I was too eager to play brat, and closed my eyes.

"On your stomach, as comfortable as you can."

With my eyes closed, I turned and leaned forward until I was on my stomach with my arms at my sides and my head turned to the side against the rug. I wiggled my butt to get comfortable.

The first place I felt it was ironically that same ass. A heat so deliciously and dangerously hot that goosebumps formed on every inch of me glided across one of my ass cheeks. The flames made contact with my skin for a fraction of a second, causing no real pain, only exhilaration. As the flames flicked over my other ass cheek, once, then twice, my toes curled.

Memories of bringing my hand as close to a candle as I could and quickly pulling it away crossed me. It was like that, only better.

I hadn't realized I was holding my breath until the heat crawled up my back from my tail bone to my shoulder blades and I exhaled strictly so I could gasp.

Hale drew quick circles on my back, curving and swirling quickly with the fire at her fingertips. I wanted to look so bad, but I didn't. Instead, I screwed my eyes shut tighter and tried to imagine it.

I could imagine her face, focused but tantalized and aroused. Her hands dancing along my flesh, taking care not to burn me.

The heat grew stronger by a fraction, just enough for me to notice, and I panted for breath, so worked up over something I could have never guessed I would be.

Between my thighs was soaked and dampening the carpet beneath me. I squirmed and squeezed my thighs together.

"You're so wet," Hale husked. "Your skin is such a lovely shade of pink, fading from the heat, do you know that?"

I shivered and my fingers curled into fists for a second, but it hurt, so I relaxed them.

"Hale," I said breathlessly.

The fire moved to my arms. It was less intense, but hot all the same. Her fingers moved in quick up and down motions, following the curve of my upper arm to my elbow, forearm and my wrist, down my fingers. My core tightened as the fire touched my palms.

The muscles she graced with her fire relaxed, while others tightened and clenched in desire.

My nipples were hard underneath me, and I whined. It seemed to go on forever, moving on from my arms to my legs down to the soles of my feet, but I had no actual idea of how time was passing.

As her hands made their way to my ass again, I was squirming and panting with need.

"H-Hale, Mistress," I pleaded, "I need you. Please."

The fire left me, and two hot fire-free hands shifted underneath me and turned me onto my back. My breasts rose and fell as I sucked in air, and my nipples only grew harder as the air surrounded them. Finally, I opened my eyes.

I watched as Hale stripped her clothing and sunk down between my thighs. Her tongue left a warm trail from my belly button to my breasts, where she kissed and lapped at one of my nipples eagerly.

"Yes," I panted.

As her lips traveled upward and finally made it to mine, she didn't kiss me hurriedly. Her lips captured mine in slow sensual movements as her tongue searched for entrance. I parted my lips with a gasp and let her tongue become one with my own.

I arched up against her, my naked breasts pressed flush to her own larger ones. My hands explored the muscles of her back and my thighs, spread wide, squeezed her.

I felt antsy and needy beneath her, but even as I whined and squirmed, she continued to kiss me tortuously slow. My wet cunt was pressed against her stomach and I rocked my hips, looking for pressure and friction.

"So needy, my Little One," she purred into my mouth. "My heart."

My entire body was flush with heat. "Please," I begged. "I need to feel you."

It felt like it had been so long since that night in the clearing when I had given myself to her. When I had tasted her juices, and felt her clit against mine and inside of me.

Hale's mouth parted from mine, leaving my lips swollen and pink around the edges. She kissed down my jawline to my neck where the scar of her bite was, and licked at every single uneven ridge of skin, lavishing it with love and attention.

I moaned and desperately rocked against her, my thighs on fire and my clit pulsing.

"Do you want me, huh?" Hale asked, grunting into my shoulder as my nails bit into her back. "My precious little mate, my dirty little girl." She continued to praise me in low, barely audible growls as I panted out her name and "yes" thrice.

Finally, she slid until her breasts were in my face, and her groin was aligned with mine. She sunk down against me fully, and her wet arousal mingled with mine.

I moaned and tilted my head back more against the rug as she thrusted slow and deep. Her hard clit pressed just against my slit and her mound rubbed against my clit so perfectly.

I felt her shiver as her clit entered me to that shallow depth and I gripped her tighter.

Hale's hands slipped onto my thighs and hips and pushed my legs up and back until my thighs were at a 90-degree angle. This position opened my pussy up to her more, and she sunk deeper into me with a grunt. My hands slipped to her shoulders, as that was all I could reach now. I clawed and struggled to grip onto her.

I cried out as I came in an instant without warning, my cunt clenching against her short length as I dripped around it.

"Good Girl," Hale growled, her thrusts becoming harder but no faster. "Give it to me, give me your pleasure. Let me feast on it." She rubbed her pussy into mine, deeper and rougher. Her voice grew more desperate and breathless. I could feel her orgasm shiver and buck against me. Her clit throbbed inside of me and she growled and grunted in the same breath.

I gasped as her claws bit into my skin, but sunk no deeper than the very surface.

Pleasure coiled in my groin and stomach, aching and throbbing. I couldn't help but moan out in breathless cries that filled the library.

"That's it," Hale moaned.

I squeezed my eyes shut. "Oh, Hale, yes...please don't stop!"

Her thrusts and rubbing grew rougher and less controlled. She pushed harder against my legs as though she was trying to get as deep as possible inside of me.

"Oh, fucking hells, my mate," she gasped, "Renee... If I could fill you with seed, I would fill you so fucking deep."

This sent me over the edge again. My hips and legs twitched

aggressively as my pussy clenched. My juices gushed between us and dripped down my ass.

"Hale!" I cried.

Suddenly, in the same second that my orgasm was dying down, Hale was setting me down and leaning back.

"Taste me," she panted. "It's what you wanted." She was shivering, and her hips were bucking against the air as she struggled to hold back.

My legs were wobbly and my mind a dizzy, foggy place, but I practically hurled myself forward and between her thighs as she leaned back on her arms. I plunged my tongue into her pussy and moaned at the musky, perfect taste. I ran my hand through her juices and caressed her.

Hale rocked her hips against me, and I knew she needed more. I switched my hand and tongue quickly. I took her clit into my mouth and pushed four of my fingers into her with ease. My hand was going to hurt even more than it already did later, but I didn't care.

"Ah!" Hale's hips bucked into me and she stiffened, her mouth silent as she came again. Her silky walls tightened around my fingers, once, then twice, and a third time until finally I could pull my fingers from her. I continued to lap slow and gentle at her clit for another few seconds.

Hale fell to her back, and I crawled on top of her. I kissed up the center of her cleavage to her chin and then finally her lips.

I kissed her slow and ardent, my heart full of love, my head full of fuzzy words I couldn't get out of my mouth right that second.

She kissed me back in equal measure until I pulled back and let myself collapse with my head nestled into the crook of her neck.

We laid like this for some time—until the flames were dim in the fireplace. Hale lifted one of my hands and started to massage it with the pads of her fingers, and I just smiled as I watched through half-open eyes.

"I love you," Hale rumbled. The words sent my heart squeezing.

"I love you too," I whispered into her neck. "I don't regret being here, I need you to know that."

Hale kissed my forehead. "Thank you."

With that, I relaxed against her body, absolutely certain that I would love Hale, forever.

"You know, I never did get that cake."